MISS PO

D0069047

RICHARD MALTBY JR. is a highly acclaimed writer and director of stage musicals. He conceived and directed *Fosse* (1999) and *Ain't Misbehavin'* (1978), both of which won Tony Awards as Best Musical, and the latter of which won him a personal Tony Award as Best Director. With long-time collaborator, composer David Shire, he directed and/or wrote lyrics for *Starting Here, Starting Now* (1977), *Baby* (1983), *Closer Than Ever* (1989) and the musical *Big* (1996). With the team of Alain Boublil and Claude-Michel Schonberg, he wrote lyrics for the international hit, *Miss Saigon* (1990), and directed and co-wrote with Don Black the American adaptation of Andrew Lloyd Webber's *Song & Dance* (1986). Most recently he conceived and directed the Johnny Cash musical, *Ring of Fire* (2006). The son of a well-known American bandleader, Richard Maltby also contributes devilish cryptic crossword puzzles to *Harpers Magazine*. He is married to Janet Brenner and has five children.

Richard Maltby became interested in writing about Beatrix Potter in 1991 when, on vacation and looking for something to read to his children, he came upon a book of Beatrix Potter stories on a hotel's bookshelf. A brief biography of the author on the cover told the story of a spinster in her thirties who fell in love after she decided to send her children's tales out into the world to be published, and who then encountered a tragic loss. She moved to the Lake District, where she married. After which (the biography said), Beatrix Potter stopped writing stories. It was this last sentence that caught Maltby's eye. Why, he thought, when a writer finally marries happily does she give up writing? One would expect the opposite, that she would write as never before. He was intrigued, and decided to try to find out what kind of woman Beatrix Potter really was. From these investigations came his first novel and screenplay, *Miss Potter*.

MISS POTTER

A NOVEL

Richard Maltby Jr.

F. WARNE & CO.

The pictures in the colour insert are taken from the movie MISS POTTER starring Renée Zellweger and Ewan McGregor, directed by Chris Noonan. A Phoenix Pictures presentation of a David Kirschner Production. Photos by Alex Bailey.

Richard Maltby Jr. wrote both the screenplay of the film and this novel.

FREDERICK WARNE

Published by Penguin Group
Penguin Group (USA) Inc., 345 Hudson Street, New York, New York 10014, U.S.A.
Penguin Group (Canada), 90 Eglinton Avenue East, Suite 700, Toronto, Ontario, Canada
M4P 2Y3 (a division of Pearson Penguin Canada Inc.)
Penguin Books Ltd, 80 Strand, London WC2R 0RL, England
Penguin Ireland, 25 St Stephen's Green, Dublin 2, Ireland
(a division of Penguin Books Ltd)
Penguin Group (Australia), 250 Camberwell Road, Camberwell, Victoria 3124, Australia
(a division of Pearson Australia Group Pty Ltd)
Penguin Books India Pvt Ltd, 11 Community Centre, Panchsheel Park,
New Delhi – 110 017, India
Penguin Group (NZ), Cnr Airborne and Rosedale Roads, Albany, Auckland 1310,
New Zealand (a division of Pearson New Zealand Ltd)
Penguin Books (South Africa) (Pty) Ltd, 24 Sturdee Avenue, Rosebank, Johannesburg 2196,
South Africa

Penguin Books Ltd, Registered Offices: 80 Strand, London WC2R 0RL, England

Web site at: www.peterrabbit.com

First published by Frederick Warne in 2006

1 3 5 7 9 10 8 6 4 2

ISBN-13: 978-0-7232-5899-5
ISBN-10: 0-7232-5899-6

Printed in U.S.A.

For Janet
and Nicholas, David, Jordan, Emily, and Charlotte

Chapter One

It is a Wonder, really – one of the great Wonders, as William Heelis used to say – how the course of a person's life can be altered, utterly and completely, by a moment so innocent one may not even notice that it has happened.

For Miss Potter, the moment came with a remark of such casualness that it seemed at the time nothing more than a passing politeness. Over the years, Miss Potter had taken to sending the children of some of her family's friends and relatives, or the children of a former governess, a story she had made up, about an animal or some such, which she illustrated in a letter with a few drawings or watercolors. They were "little" stories, and they usually didn't have any particular point, no moral or anything dull like that. They were intended to make children smile. If the children were sick, the story might make them feel better. If it were their birthday, the story was a special present that would help to make them remember that they had a maiden aunt Beatrix, and that she was fond of them.

On this particular day, Miss Potter showed one of her stories to an old family friend, Canon Rawnsley, vicar in the Lake District village where the Potter family often spent their summers. It was the "Tale" of a naughty rabbit who trespassed into a garden he was forbidden to visit. Beatrix had had the story printed, privately, as a gift for friends. Canon Rawnsley was quite taken by it. In fact (since nothing Canon Rawnsley ever did was subtle), his laughter boomed through the house. He asked if Beatrix had written any more. As it happened, Beatrix had sketches of several of her "letter" stories. "These are delightful," Canon Rawnsley announced to the entire universe when he had finished them. Then came the sentence that was to change Miss Potter's life. "You should publish them," he said.

Miss Potter brushed aside the compliment. The stories had no "importance". They were gifts for friends – for children at that. They hadn't been worked over or edited – although of course, Canon Rawnsley was very kind to have said he enjoyed them.

Canon Rawnsley stopped and had, for him, a very uncharacteristic moment of silence. "It happens that I know a book publisher. Why don't I make an inquiry?" And there it was. The moment had come, and passed, and no one in the room had noticed.

But that is how it happened that several months later, Miss Helen Beatrix Potter, aged thirty-six, found herself seated at a large table in a publishing house watching two dour businessmen snuffle and snort as they pored over her portfolio of drawings and writings. Miss Potter had never been to a place of business before. She seldom went anywhere beyond the small circle of her life. And of course she never went anywhere alone. Miss Wiggin, her chaperone, in her sixties and preternaturally gloomy, accompanied her everywhere, and even now sat motionless in a small chair near the door.

Beatrix's trip to the offices of F. Warne and Co. had not started well. The Potter carriage arrived at Bedford Street, in London's Covent Garden, on a spring day in 1902. Saunders, the coachman, jumped to the street and opened the door. Inside, the blinds had been drawn. "Miss Potter," Saunders said, to the darkened interior, "we're here."

"Quite," said Beatrix.

It took her several moments to summon the courage to move. Then, swallowing hard, she took her portfolio in hand. "Come, everyone," she said. "Come, Miss Wiggin."

The Georgian building had a front door bearing a brass plate that read: "F. Warne & Co. Book Publishers". Saunders opened it. A roomful of Uriah Heeps working at tall desks looked up. Women seldom entered these premises.

"Miss Potter to see the Messrs Warne," said Miss Potter to a man seated by the door. "I'm the deliveryman," said the man. "You want over there."

The deliveryman indicated a desk across the room, at which sat an important-looking man in a black suit. Beatrix addressed this man. "I have an appointment. I believe Canon Rawnsley was kind enough to write to you. I've brought the manuscript, as you can see." The man looked at her blankly. "I'm sorry," said Miss Potter. "Which Mr. Warne do I have the honor of addressing?"

"You have the honor of addressing Messrs Warne's secretary. And you are?"

"Beatrix Potter. *Miss* Potter."

The man gave her a long look. What he saw before him was a perfect "unmarried lady": hair drawn back, dress tight-laced and sexless – not an unattractive woman, but her every physical virtue toned down, tied back or hidden.

"Of course," the secretary said ambiguously. He rose and opened the door. "*Miss* Potter," he announced to the room inside. Beatrix and Miss Wiggin walked past him and the secretary closed the door behind them. He rolled his eyes. "*Miss* Potter, indeed!"

So it was that by the time she sat watching Harold and Fruing Warne pore through her portfolio, Miss Potter was already feeling ridiculous and out-of-place. Why had she come? Why had she even allowed Canon Rawnsley to make his "inquiry"?

She looked at the two brothers: cheerless, unsmiling men – adult males with not a whit of humor – passing around her small watercolors of animals, which Beatrix now realized must look absurdly fey.

"Hmmm," said Harold Warne.

"Hmmm," said his brother Fruing.

"Hmmph," snorted Harold.

"Garrumph," echoed Fruing, twitching his nose.

Beatrix knew she should sit quietly while her fate was being sealed, but . . . they were judging her! I must look such an amateur, she thought. She had to speak.

"I have been selling my drawings for greeting cards, place cards, et cetera, for over ten years. I believe I am fully professional," she said, and held out a small hand-painted gift card. Neither man took it.

"I had a governess as a child, then two private tutors. Other than that, I am largely self-taught," Beatrix offered, instantly regretting it, for she had now defined herself as an amateur.

The brothers had divided Beatrix's work into two piles. Occasionally one would pass a drawing to the other. Harold passed Fruing a picture of a rabbit wearing a blue jacket. Fruing responded by clearing his throat.

Light shining in from the side window caught Fruing's bushy side-whiskers, and Harold's trimmed beard, giving both their heads a frame that almost looked like fur. With their curious snuffling noises, garrumphs, tsks, wheezes and clucks, and their hairy silhouettes, from Beatrix's perspective the two men suddenly looked like, well . . . animals – a badger or a hedgehog perhaps. It occurred to Beatrix that they might make a drawing. In her mind she began to sketch them: two animal friends living in a hole by a river bed. A cozy, well furnished home under a tree-root, perhaps, with a carpet and a fireplace and a . . .

Beatrix shook the thought from her head.

The brothers exchanged more pages: a rabbit squeezing through a hole in a fence, a rabbit running through a vegetable garden, a rabbit hiding in a watering can. "Bunnies in jackets with brass buttons. However do you imagine such things?" Harold Warne muttered without looking up.

"Oh, I don't imagine them. I see them. They're quite real. They're my friends."

"Ah! You base the animal characters on your friends."

"Oh no. The animals *are* my friends. Sometimes, I'm afraid, my only friends. Before Peter Rabbit, there was Benjamin H. Bouncer. And Sir Isaac the Newt. I have their drawings too. Would you care to see them?" Beatrix produced another small packet from her bag.

"That won't be necessary," said Harold Warne, closing Beatrix's portfolio with an ominous finality. He forced his face into a smile. "Unfortunately, Miss Potter . . . It is *Miss* Potter, is it not?" He looked at her again. "Yes, how silly of me. Unfortunately, the market for children's stories . . ."

Beatrix did not wish to hear more. She could feel the

walls of this small office closing in on her. She plumped her drawings back into a neat pile, and all she could think was: how quickly can I get out of this room, without being unforgivably rude? Her quick mind tried to calculate the precise degree of rudeness that might be socially acceptable, because rudeness of some kind had become unavoidable. She was going to flee. "I understand completely. It was foolish of me to come. I am inexperienced in the world of business, and . . ."

At the table, Fruing Warne turned in his chair, and interrupted his brother. "F. Warne and Co. would like to publish your little book, Miss Potter."

Harold Warne's jaw dropped open. "We would?" he said.

Miss Potter looked from one brother to the next.

"There's something quite sweet about this story," Fruing continued. "You say you sold out your private printing?"

"Two hundred and fifty copies," said Beatrix. "I gave most of them as gifts, but I put some in a local bookshop and they sold them all."

"I'll assign it to one of our partners, and send our solicitor to arrange the details."

"How . . . well, I'm . . . very . . ." stammered Beatrix.

Fruing Warne leaned forward and produced a smile only slightly less forced than his brother's. In time, Beatrix would come to refer to this as the "Warne smile". "Don't get too hopeful, Miss Potter. I know publishing. Your book won't sell a great number of copies. But I think we can have a small profit."

Beatrix suddenly could not control her hands. They fluttered this way and that. "My dear Mr. Warne. I shall do everything possible to ensure that you have not made a mistake. Well, I'm . . . pleased. Very pleased. Indeed." She gave her hands the task of putting her drawings back into her portfolio, which seemed to still them. She stood up. "Miss Wiggin, I believe we can go now. Thank you so much, Messrs Warne, for your time."

Harold Warne moved to the office door and held it open for her. "Our pleasure," he said, and looked back at the table. "My brother always . . . knows what he's doing."

Miss Potter started to go out of the door, but a thought that had haunted her from the moment Canon Rawnsley had told her the name of the firm he was recommending now came tumbling out. "I'm quite particular about book size and price. And color. Rather than that dreary brown wash your children's books usually have, I'd really much prefer black and white. And I would also like to avoid that dreadful Gothic typeface you use."

Harold Warne, holding the door, froze. The brown wash and Gothic typeface were the hallmark of F. Warne and Co. children's books, and were probably the reason why they were popular. Beyond that, he, Harold, had personally chosen the quaint sepia tint, and thought it and the typeface together gave the books a charming timelessness. If this woman, this Miss Potter, didn't like the Warne publishing style, why was she here? He gave Beatrix another Warne smile.

"I'm sure everything will be to your satisfaction," he said. Anything to get her out of the room.

Fruing called from the table, "Miss Potter. Your . . ."

"My drawings. Of course. Thank you so much."

Beatrix returned to the table and picked up the portfolio

Harold had been perusing. Fruing Warne was holding her printed edition of "The Tale of Peter Rabbit". She reached out for it. "Come along, Peter," she said.

She turned, summoned the glum Miss Wiggin, and left the room.

Harold dropped his head against the door. "English spinsters. God, what a breed! London must have a million of them – each with a watercolor set on Saturday afternoons, and a pet to receive all that unused love. No surprise they all go dotty. Sir Isaac the Newt!"

"Wait till you get one in negotiation. You'll see how dotty they are."

"You can't be serious, Fruing. That book won't sell ten copies."

"Of course not. However, the thought did occur to me . . ."

Suddenly Fruing's odd behavior became clear.

"Norman!" the brothers exclaimed in one voice.

Outside the window, they could see Miss Potter and Miss Wiggin approaching their carriage.

Fruing Warne smiled at his own cleverness. "We promised our little brother a project. If he mucks this up, it will hardly matter. And he's a genius with "ladies of a certain age". I think Miss Potter may be a godsend."

~

Outside the publishing house, Saunders helped Beatrix and Miss Wiggin into the waiting carriage.

"Home, Miss Beatrix?"

Beatrix stopped. Her body felt a sensation totally new

to her. She wasn't sure what it was exactly. But suddenly the thought of merely returning home seemed … unthinkable. "No, Saunders," she said. "Ride me through the Park. Through all the parks!"

Saunders was shocked. Miss Potter never varied her schedule. "I beg your pardon, miss. Are you sure?"

"Drive!"

Saunders leapt to his seat and the carriage lurched into motion.

Inside the carriage, Beatrix opened her portfolio.

"I did it!" she said. "Did you hear my heart? It was a kettle drum!"

Miss Wiggin, sitting unobtrusively in the seat corner, looked up at her odd mistress. Miss Wiggin did not like the Potter family. She had been raised in splendor as a child, but long ago her family's fortune had disappeared and she had been forced to go to work. Of the several positions she had had over the years, this was the best-paid and most secure, but she wondered often if it was worth the price. A lady of the house who tolerated not the tiniest infraction, and a spinster daughter who . . . talked to her own drawings!

Indeed, there she was, right across the carriage, conversing with her sketchpad!

"See, my friends. It is as Canon Rawnsley said. We can't stay home quietly all our life. We must present ourselves to people. We must look upon it as an adventure. And see – they liked us!"

Beatrix took out a pencil and a clean sheet of paper – and began to draw. "Peter, Jeremy, Jemima, everyone: look who I just met."

The rhythmic clip-clop of the horse's hooves on the pavement became a kind of musical accompaniment to the ride. Against it, Beatrix's pencil flicked over the page and in an instant she had produced a sketch of two animals who looked amazingly like Harold and Fruing Warne. "Once upon a time," said Beatrix, "in a place of business in London, there lived two . . . um, businessmen. Who made odd snuffling noises whenever they felt . . ." She put down the pencil.

"I don't think these two are going to make a story. Oh, Miss Wiggin, look at this day!"

The carriage traveled through the gates of Hyde Park into glorious gardens which sparkled in the crisp sunlight of this breathtaking spring day. Inside, Beatrix looked at the glum Miss Wiggin, and then at the scene through the window.

"What a glorious day!" she cried. "A glorious day to get some air!"

Beatrix struggled with the carriage window, and finally slid it open. Wiggin frowned. As if in response, Beatrix leaned her head and shoulders entirely out of the window.

"Faster, Saunders, if you please! Faster!"

Miss Wiggin was appalled. "No, Miss Beatrix! No! Someone will see!"

But Beatrix was not to be dissuaded. The wind whipped at her face. The trees flashed past as the carriage sped though the magnificent grandeur of London on a perfect day. It is spring, thought Beatrix, beaming. Everything is a metaphor.

The carriage emerged from Hyde Park, and in short

order arrived at the Potter home at Number 2 Bolton Gardens. Saunders jumped down, opened the carriage door, helped Beatrix and Miss Wiggin to the street, and then attended to the horses. Beatrix, humming merrily to herself, proceeded up the walk.

Inside the house, Beatrix's mother, Mrs. Helen Potter, a woman just past sixty, was doing needlepoint in the morning room. Mrs. Potter was once, if not beautiful, at least vivacious, but years of disappointment had hardened her features so that now she appeared plain and severe. She didn't look up as Beatrix entered the house almost dancing, heading straight for the staircase, but simply called out, "It's past four. Where have you been?"

Beatrix called back from the stairs unnaturally loudly, since it had become obvious in recent years that, despite her mother's protestations to the contrary, she was becoming hard-of-hearing. "I'm a thirty-six-year-old woman! I can do things without permission from my mother!"

"Precisely," Mrs. Potter called back. "You hardly need me to tell you what is seemly and what is not. Your father came home early from the club again. Another headache."

On the staircase, Beatrix stopped.

"The stonemason arrived for the garden wall," Mrs. Potter went on, "and with you gone no one knew what he was to do. And Bertram has reappeared. He's in his room sleeping. Perhaps before dinner you can elicit some information on where he's been. Where were you?"

"I took a drive . . ." said Beatrix.

Mrs. Potter raised her voice thunderously. "Speak up! You know it makes me irritable when I can't hear you."

Beatrix, on the stairs, sighed. There was no way she

could speak louder. "I took a drive . . ." she said at the same volume, ". . . with my friends!" She continued up the stairs.

Beatrix arrived at the second floor landing and started towards the staircase to her studio. Along the way, she passed her brother's room which she rarely entered since Bertram was seldom home. She knocked and, hearing nothing, opened the door.

The curtains were drawn. The room was lit by a few streaks of daylight that had managed to slip through the cracks. Walter Bertram Potter, Beatrix's brother, aged twenty-nine, good-looking in a disheveled sort of way, was lying on the bed fully dressed, snoring – a silver flask in his hand.

"Bertie . . ." Beatrix whispered.

On the bed, Bertram opened one eye.

"Hullo, Bee," he said. "I'm not asleep."

Beatrix forced herself to sound irritated. "We've been worried sick. Where on earth have you . . . ?"

"Later," said Bertram. "If anyone asks, I'm still sleeping it off. Shh!" He took a swig from his flask and fell back into the pillow, feigning passing out.

Beatrix smiled down at him. She could never stay angry at Bertram, not when he started play-acting. That was their entire childhood together.

She leaned close to the bed. "Bertie . . ." she said. "They liked it."

"Ripping!" said Bertram opening his eyes. "Bee, I'm going back to Scotland in the morning. Can I steal your pastels? I'm out." He closed his eyes again.

Beatrix straightened up. After all these years, she still

wasn't used to Bertram disappointing her.

"Of course," she said, walking to the door.

"Shh!" said Bertram from the bed, eyes closed.

Beatrix closed the door behind her.

Down the hall was her parents' room.

Rupert Potter, sixty-nine years old, with a mane of grey hair and majestic sideburns, was seated in the semi-dark, a wet towel folded across his eyes. The curtains were drawn in this room too.

"How are you feeling, Father? Shall I change your compress?" Beatrix took the towel from his eyes and wet it in a basin on the chiffonier.

Rupert barely moved. "The partnership sent a contract round to the club for me to review. Be a good girl and send Wilkinson a message that I can't possibly."

Beatrix squeezed the water out of the towel. "Why do they send you contracts? You don't review them. I've never seen you review one ever."

"I'm a figurehead," Rupert said dryly. This was Rupert's sense of humor. One had to have lived with him a long time to recognize it.

"Would it hurt terribly if I opened the curtains?" said Beatrix.

"Yes!" said Rupert.

Beatrix reapplied the compress. "I went to F. Warne and Co. today."

Rupert put his hand to his temple, and grimaced in pain.

"Shh! Later," he said.

Beatrix didn't continue. "It's the phosphorus, Father. You heard what the Doctor said. The flash powder gives

19

you headaches. No more indoor photographs."

Rupert waved a hand. "Do you like those on the bed?"

The bed was covered with photographs that Rupert Potter had just developed: nature studies, pictures of people with interesting faces that he had passed on the street and persuaded to pose for him. The photos were perfectly cropped. They were more than photographs. They were art.

"Very nice," said Beatrix, and tiptoed out of the room.

The staircase continued up to the third floor. At the top landing was the door to a room that had once been the nursery but which Beatrix had converted into her bedroom and studio.

Her room was filled with paintings and drawings of animals. Sketches of her story characters adorned the walls. Shelves were lined with artifacts from her childhood that she couldn't bear to part with: an animal skull, a microscope, Bertram's first collection of butterflies and moths. In the center of the room Beatrix had put together several desks and a drawing board, which was her studio. Off to the side, up a few more steps, was the small room under the eaves that housed her bed.

Beatrix spoke to a drawing of a rabbit. "Oh, Benjamin! Look at me! I'm going to be an author!" She turned to another drawing. "And you, Peter – you are going to be published!" Was it just a trick of the light, or did the rabbit in the blue jacket on the page wiggle its nose in delight?

Behind her, Mrs. Potter entered the room, ready to reprimand her wastrel son severely. "So, Bertram, you've decided to grace us with your . . ."

Mrs. Potter stopped. She looked around the room:

Beatrix was alone. "I wish you wouldn't talk to yourself, Beatrix. It makes you seem odd."

"I just do it for company," Beatrix replied.

Mrs. Potter barreled ahead. "And who were these friends you were out with all day? I know your friends. You don't have any."

Beatrix opened her paintbox. "Yes I do, Mother. Every time I paint."

Mrs. Potter had long ago given up trying to educate her daughter about the world, but every now and then she fell into the trap and made one more attempt. "Some of your paintings are quite pretty, Beatrix, but I'm not going to deceive you as your father does and call them art."

Beatrix didn't look up. She dipped her brush in a paint pot.

There seemed nothing more for Mrs. Potter to say. "Tut," she said, and left the room.

Beatrix leaned over her new drawing to a framed painting of the rabbit in a blue jacket.

"Well, my friend," she said to Peter Rabbit, "when I'm a published author, then we shall see."

Chapter Two

If someone could have waved a magic wand and taken Beatrix back twenty-five years in time, she would have been found in this very room, for it had been the nursery of the Potter children ever since Beatrix was born. Rupert's family was from Manchester, his wife, Helen Leech, from a town nearby. The couple married in Manchester, but immediately took up residence in London, in Upper Harley Street before the street became famous for its doctors. When they found they were expecting their first child, they bought a grand home in Bolton Gardens, a newly built square of four-storey houses in a very fashionable country-like area of Kensington. This was to be Beatrix's home for almost forty years.

As was generally the case in Victorian England, the children were hidden away in a pleasant room on the top floor, one with sloping ceilings and dormer windows that looked out onto the street. Up a few steps was a small extra room where Nurse slept – Nurse Fiona McKenzie, a formidable young woman from the Scottish Highlands who firmly believed in the existence of fairies and witches. When Beatrix grew to adulthood, she was given a large bedroom on the second floor, but it was very formal, and she quickly converted the nursery into a place to which she could retire to draw and paint. In time she even moved her bed into the small side room intended for the nursemaid.

The studio was cozy. It was gas lit. It had a fireplace. When it was a nursery, it had two small beds, pink wallpaper with a flower design, and shelves and shelves for toys and books and artifacts. There was a large dollhouse that was a replica of 2 Bolton Gardens, filled with miniature furniture that had been hand-made by a craftsman in Knightsbridge who only worked for the best people and who, rather significantly, accepted a commission from the Potters. What distinguished this room from other nurseries was that it was also filled with animals. The rabbit cage that now stood empty near Beatrix's drawing desk was there twenty-five years earlier in the same spot, but then there was a rabbit in it, whom the children had named Benjamin H. Bouncer. Nearby were two more rabbit cages, a cage of mice (whom the children had named Tom Thumb and Hunca Munca), a run with a white rat in it, a terrarium with salamanders and a newt (Sir Isaac the . . .), a birdcage with a jaybird, several fish bowls, a butterfly-and-insect collection, and several bottles containing live insects. There were also stuffed animals, animal skeletons (which Beatrix spent hours drawing), and countless accurate sketches of animal anatomy, some of which were gifts to the children from a family friend in the Royal Academy of Science. There were also, but less importantly, toys: tin soldiers, dolls, miniature trains. In short this room was the ideal setting for two picture-perfect but rather quirky Victorian children.

In December of 1876, Beatrix, aged ten, sat drawing Benjamin H. Bouncer in the notebook she devoted entirely to him. She studied the rabbit, then drew with great intensity and accuracy. But, curiously, in her drawing she kept having the impulse to draw the rabbit clothed.

Nurse called from the lavatory down the hall. "Beatrix, Bertram, time for your bath."

Beatrix didn't look up. "I'm not finished."

Nurse would have none of it. "With your parents leaving at seven, you most certainly are. Come along, Bertram."

Bertram, four years old, soft brown hair curling around his brow, a classic angel, was pinning a live moth into his insect collection. "Wait! Wait! Just one more minute!" he said. "There! I got him."

"Bertram, you're barbaric," said Beatrix, putting down her pen.

Before long, the children, bathed, immaculately dressed in bedclothes, robes and slippers, were taken by Nurse out into the hall to the long flight of stairs down to the second floor, and into the sumptuous bedroom of Mr. and Mrs. Rupert Potter.

Mr. and Mrs. Potter were in the final stages of dressing for the evening. Helen Potter at this time was thirty-seven, still attractive in a severe way, and tonight enveloped in a beautiful evening gown of champagne-colored satin. Rupert Potter, aged forty-four, was in tails. Rupert had recently responded to the new hirsute style among men of quality by growing enormous bushy sideburns that all but covered his cheeks. This seemed a response to fashion, but Rupert Potter had private reasons for enjoying the change in his look. He thought that it made him stand out when he walked in a room, gave him character. Fashion had suddenly allowed him to be "different", something that he longed for in a way even he didn't understand.

These then were the parents Beatrix encountered

when she entered their room, and an odd-looking set of contradictions they were: Helen, round-faced, sober, cheerless, but expensively and gaily dressed; and Rupert, hairy-cheeked, somber, unsmiling, but blithe and well-turned-out in his perfectly tailored evening clothes. Beatrix thought they looked radiant.

"The children, madam," Nurse announced.

"It can't be seven already," said Rupert at the mirror, feverishly attempting to tie his tie.

At this precise moment Mr. and Mrs. Potter were in a tizzy because of the time.

"For God's sake, hurry, Rupert!" said Helen. "It won't do to be late at the Hydes'. Theodora runs a dinner like a railway conductor, and she can be just as surly."

In the mirror, Rupert could see his daughter. "Doesn't your mother look beautiful, Beatrix? Being in a temper puts such a rose in her cheeks."

"When you grow up, Beatrix, and have to run a household, plan parties, buy clothing, keep a social schedule, and put up with a husband who has never been introduced to a clock, your cheeks will glow too." Mrs. Potter's eye landed on Beatrix for one second. "What is that loose ribbon in Beatrix's collar?"

Nurse leapt to examine the collar for the almost imperceptible flaw.

"It's very unsightly," continued Mrs. Potter. "Change her into something else, and give that nightdress away."

At the mirror, Rupert's tie had come out wrong, one end far too long for balance.

"Well, this won't do," he muttered. "One more try."

Mrs. Potter had reached her limit. "You're impossible!

We are so late!" She grabbed the tie out of his hands and started tying it for him. "Do you think it was easy getting this invitation? Our reputation will be nil."

Rupert, standing rigid as his wife worked at his collar, tried to reclaim some dignity by conversing with his daughter. "And what have you drawn today, Beatrix?"

"Don't encourage her, Rupert," said Mrs. Potter. "Remember our talk."

Beatrix held up her sketchbook. "Benjamin Bouncer, eating lettuce."

Rupert looked at her drawing with his eyes only, trying successfully not to move his head at all. "The paws are getting better and better."

"Rupert!" Mrs. Potter exclaimed. She stepped back, having finished the tie. "There. Done. And now . . . we go!"

Nurse knew it was time to move quickly. "Say your goodnights, children," she said, herding them into a formal row. Beatrix curtsied to each of her parents. "Goodnight, Mother. Goodnight, Father." Bertram stepped forward and shook each of his parents' hands. "Goodnight, Mother. Goodnight, sir."

Mrs. Potter kissed them quickly. "Goodnight, Beatrix. Goodnight, Bertram. You're very good children. Now hurry upstairs." Gwendolyn, her lady's maid, stepped forward with Mrs. Potter's rather magnificent satin evening coat, tailored to match the champagne-colored gown.

Nurse prodded the children like a Scottish sheepdog. "Come along now. Mustn't make your mother and father . . ."

". . . later than they are!" cried Mrs. Potter, leaving the room and flying down the stairs.

In the front hall, Cox, the butler, was helping Rupert into his overcoat. "Oh, children," Rupert said suddenly.

Helen Potter could not believe it. "What now?" she exclaimed.

Rupert took two packages from his coat pocket. "On my way home, I happened to walk through Harrods, and when I got to the street, guess what seems to have jumped into my pocket?"

"Not more drawing pencils, Rupert! Really!"

"No, my dearest. That's all finished – as we agreed. These are something very suitable for a young lady who will soon grow up to run a fine house just like her mother."

Beatrix and Bertram ran down the stairs to receive their presents.

Nurse clapped from the upper landing. "We shall open them upstairs. Up. Up."

"Thank you, Father," said Beatrix and Bertram in unison, and they turned and raced up the stairs.

At the landing, Beatrix stopped and looked back down at her parents. Her mother, shimmering in satin, hair piled high, bejeweled, perfumed, attended by her personal maid, did not look like her mother; she shone like a princess from the books of fairy stories Beatrix had in her room. Her father, powerful and secure, slim pants under his fine coat, looked dashing – and when he donned his sleek top hat, he became a creature of magic, a savior, a modern Prince Charming. Gazing down upon them, Beatrix thought her parents were pure Romance.

"Come, Rupert!" cried Mrs. Potter, and the two swept through the doorway into the street.

Beatrix raced upstairs, entered the nursery, ran to the window, and looked down.

The street outside had been transformed by a blanket of snow. The Potters' carriage awaited, brass trimmings shimmering from the pools of gaslight, Saunders the coachman on the bench, a footman at the carriage door.

Beatrix was an imaginative ten-year-old girl, but in truth not so much more imaginative than other sequestered girls her age. Growing up tucked away in a nursery, with books and toys her only contact with the world, Beatrix had a mind that had been shaped by fantasy in a way adults of her parents' generation would never understand.

Beatrix looked down at the waiting carriage, and in her young mind, what she saw was a golden coach drawn by three pairs of white rabbits, with a mouse in a coachman's coat sitting on the bench, another in footman's clothes at the carriage door, and other mice attendants holding candelabra.

Mr. and Mrs. Potter swept down the walk like fanciful animals in a picture book: Mrs. Potter, an opulently dressed Persian cat, Mr. Potter, a regally dressed dandified prince of a frog. It would have been a scene of perfect magic had it not been accompanied by the sound of her parents squabbling unpleasantly all the way to the coach.

"Late! Late! Late!"

"We are not late!"

"We've never been invited to the Hydes'. I doubt we'll be invited again!"

"If not, it won't my fault."

"What is that supposed to mean?"

"Get in the carriage!"

"You're stepping on my coat!"

Behind her, Bertram's voice broke the mood. "Click beetles! Father found them for me! And there's just room in my specimen collection!"

Bertram had opened his gift package and taken out three huge dead insects, each about two inches long, and now, at a large shadow box filled with butterflies and moths, he brandished a long thick pin.

"Bertram, you assassin!" said Beatrix.

"Open your present," Bertram said, as with a grunt, he impaled the first beetle with one joyous jab.

Beatrix opened her present. It was a set of ceramic food plates for a dollhouse: dinner plates with meals served, a platter with a ham, a bowl of fruit, puddings. Beatrix understood the gift immediately. "China. With food on it. Well, this should help me to be a silly woman who runs a household. If that's what everyone wants."

She went to the dollhouse, opened the front wall and carefully placed the dishes on the dining-room table. She put two dolls into dining-room chairs.

"Lucinda, Jane, look at what's for dinner? Much better than what I usually serve you, which is nothing at all."

Nurse had turned down the beds. "Come, children. One story, then off to sleep."

"I want Beatrix to tell a story," said Bertram, his skewering completed. "Hers are funny."

Beatrix smiled to herself. "Indeed they are. Now, what shall it be about?" She scanned the room and her eyes fell on the two mice in a small glass cage.

"Tom Thumb and Hunca Munca!" cried Bertram.

"Yes, Bertram, precisely."

She brought the cage over to the dollhouse, and addressed the mice. "Tom, Hunca Munca, are you ready to play roles in a story?" She assumed a little mouse voice. "Oh, yes, we're excellent actors." In her own voice again: "Well, we shall see about that. This will be your test."

She sat back, and without a moment of preparation began to make up a story.

"Once upon a time," recited Beatrix, "those excellent housekeepers, Lucinda and Jane, bought some shiny new porcelain food, which they set out on their perfectly appointed dining-room table. Then they decided to go for a walk."

She walked the two dolls out of the dollhouse, and plopped them down at a distance.

"Suddenly, there came a scuffling noise in the kitchen. Tom Thumb and Hunca Munca crept out, ravenous."

She opened the cage, took out the two mice one at a time, and set them down in the dining room of the dollhouse.

"The mice saw that the dining table was set for dinner," Beatrix continued. "Tom Thumb leapt up, took a big bite from the first plate and – hrrump – broke his tooth! Oww!"

Bertram joined her, and together they prodded the two mice until they ran about the dining table, clattering among the porcelain food, tails swinging, knocking over plates, tiny silverware and candelabra, making an impressive mess.

"Tom Thumb was enraged!" she said.

"So angry that – what, Bee?" Bertram interjected.

"Wait, Bertram, wait! I feel it coming," Beatrix said, raising her hand to stop all action.

Bertram waited.

Beatrix suddenly erupted in verse:

> "'I can't eat stone,' cried out Tom Thumb,
>   'This dinner's a disaster!
> I'll starve here waiting for the dust to settle –
>   The soup is china, the fish is metal,
> The tea is porcelain and so's the kettle,
>   And the duck is alabaster!
> Where can I get some food to eat
>   That isn't made of plaster?!'"

"How do you do that?" said Nurse, genuinely amazed.

"Do what?" asked Beatrix.

"Make up rhymes like that?"

Playing out the imaginary rage of the mice, Beatrix knocked the porcelain plates of food on to the dollhouse floor, tipping over all the chairs and candlesticks in the process.

"Crash! Smash! Ooops! Sorry! Thud!" she exclaimed.

Tom Thumb and Hunca Munca, frightened now, scurried from room to room, knocking over miniature chairs and tables, a sideboard here, a grandfather clock there. Hunca Munca mounted the staircase and proceeded to lay waste to the bedrooms, her tail sweeping into everything in sight.

Beatrix surveyed the devastation, and inspired by it, continued her verse.

"Later that night, when Lucinda and Jane
　　Returned from their evening rambles,
They found their beautiful neat domain
　　A complete and total shambles.
Which only proves one thing, I find –
　　A moral for all, my friend,
Those too concerned
　　That their house be impeccable
Soon will have learned
　　That everything's wreckable.
And neatness may seem to bring peace of mind
　　But it never will last – The End.''

Bertram groused. "That isn't much of a story," he said.

"It could be a good story," said Beatrix, with a mischievous smile. "I intend to work on it."

"It's a very naughty story, if you ask me," Nurse grumbled, tucking Bertram in. "They are very bad mice."

Beatrix locked the mice back in their glass cage. "That's because you haven't heard the ending," she said brightly, inventing on the spot. "On Christmas Eve, Tom Thumb found a sixpence on the floor, and put it in Lucinda's stocking, so he paid for everything he broke. And every morning, Hunca Munca sweeps the dolls' house with her tail and a dustpan. Good housekeeping triumphs! It's a very moral story."

Nurse turned down the gaslight. "Moral!" she said, and went up to her bedchamber.

Beatrix smiled to herself and snuggled down into her bed.

"I thought you'd like it."

Chapter Three

A jangle of bells cut through the silence of the Potter house, followed a few seconds later by the click of tight-laced servant's shoes on the marble floor of the front hall.

"Are we expecting someone?" said Mrs. Potter, looking up from her sewing. She and Beatrix were in the morning room that sat at the back of the house between the drawing room and the sunlit garden.

"It's my guests, Mother," said Beatrix, folding the napkin she was edging. "The men publishing my book." And she added, "As you well know."

Mrs. Potter liked to pretend that she was ignorant of what was happening in her house; that no one told her anything and that it was all a mystery. That was her way of controlling things, as she entered what she had decided were her declining years. Being hard-of-hearing, she had learned, was a great asset.

A look of apprehension came over Beatrix's face. "And it's not a social call. In fact, I fear it's going to be quite unpleasant."

"I wish you wouldn't invite tradespeople into the house," Mrs. Potter continued, pretending she had heard nothing. "They carry dust."

Beatrix opened the French doors and said in a voice that even a woman going deaf couldn't miss, "I would have gone to their office, Mother, but I didn't think it wise to leave you alone – as you have made quite clear!"

Beatrix entered the drawing room, chose a chair near the fireplace where tea had been set out, and perched lightly on the edge of its cushion, sitting upright in the most proper manner. She adjusted her skirt so that no wrinkles showed. In the background, she could hear noises of a visitor being admitted to the foyer. Jane, the maid, entered the room.

"Mr. Norman Warne," Jane announced, giving a name Beatrix had not heard before.

A young man entered the room.

Beatrix reacted in surprise. Mr. Norman Warne was not a dour, furry tradesman like the brothers she had met. He was a handsome young man in his mid-thirties, smartly dressed in a tweed suit, his hair short and neatly parted, his only concession to the current fashion for facial hair a neatly trimmed moustache that gave his otherwise bland features a definite dash.

Beatrix blinked.

Norman Warne gave a little bow. "Miss Potter, I hope you will forgive my intrusion into your daily routine."

"I hope you will forgive my astonishment. I was expecting one of the . . ."

Norman stepped forward. "I am . . . yes, well, I'm Harold and Fruing's younger brother. I have recently joined the firm and they have done me the honor to assign your book on rabbits to me. It was most gracious of you to invite me to, um . . . to, um . . ."

"Tea?" said Beatrix, helpfully.

"Yes, I'd love some!" said Norman, a little too

quickly and a little too loudly. Then in a calmer voice, he added, "Yes, that would be, um, quite . . . well, yes, thank you."

Norman looked around for a seat. He started to choose the divan, then changed his mind and rested on the chair beside it. He took a deep breath and announced, "Lemon."

Beatrix watched with some dismay. It was suddenly clear that young, handsome Mr. Norman Warne was shy, socially ill-at-ease, and – Beatrix could not avoid the word – a bit of a bumbler.

Behind Mr. Warne, Miss Wiggin entered the room, and sat quietly in a chair by the door.

Beatrix poured the tea. "Are there more of you, Mr. Warne? Am I to look forward to an endless parade of Warnes?" She passed Mr. Warne the cup.

"There was a fourth brother once, the eldest, Frederick, but he died when I was young. I have one sister, Edith, who has married and lives in Sussex, and another sister, Amelia, who lives at home. That is my entire family. But I expect I'm the only Warne you'll need concern yourself with from now on."

Beatrix took a sip of tea and set down her cup. She had prepared herself for this meeting, and did not want it to degenerate into conversation. "Mr. Warne, I would like to get right to the point. I received a letter from your brothers . . ."

"I don't mean to interrupt, Miss Potter," said Norman, interrupting. "But before we discuss, um, business, might I be so presumptuous as to ask, um . . . well . . ."

"Yes?" said Beatrix.

"Well, um, might it be possible to *see* the book we're publishing?"

"Oh," said Beatrix, derailed.

"My brothers have described it to me, but . . ."

"Yes, of course. I have it here on the table."

"Excellent!" said Norman. "As soon as we have finished tea . . ." he looked at his cup, ". . . which I have . . ." he placed the cup back on the tea table, ". . . we must . . . have a look." He paused. "Perhaps now."

He rose and went to the portfolio, which was bound by a neat ribbon. He stopped.

"You just untie it," said Beatrix.

Norman untied the ribbon and started to leaf through the book.

Beatrix sat back in her chair. Now! she thought to herself. Yes, now is the time to sip a cup of tea – very slowly. She picked up her cup.

Once again, Beatrix had to sit quietly while her work was being assessed. The tick of the grandfather clock in the hall echoed louder and louder. Every few moments came the tiny rustle of a page turning. But this time the silence was broken, from time to time, by actual words.

"Extraordinary!" said Norman, turning a page.

"Charming!" he said, turning another. "Enchanting." "Oh! Oh, how funny!" "Ah!" he said. "Very nice!" And he laughed out loud.

Finally Norman turned the last page. "This is delightful! Magical! And so beautifully drawn." He turned to Beatrix. "Well. Miss Potter! I'm . . . well, utterly, utterly speechless."

Beatrix was unprepared for his reaction. It was

charming, she thought. But she had resolved to be firm, even unpleasant if need be, and didn't want to be distracted. "Perhaps, Mr. Warne, we can now discuss our business?"

"I put your drawings aside with the greatest reluctance," Norman said. He closed the portfolio and brought it with him back to the chair.

Beatrix sat forward. "Mr. Warne, I'm afraid I must speak quite harshly. Your brothers' letter made two proposals which I find quite unacceptable. First, they want the drawings to be in color. I am adamant they be in black and white."

"But," said Norman, "Peter Rabbit's blue jacket. And the red radishes. Surely you want your enchanting drawings reproduced as they are?"

"Of course I would prefer color," said Beatrix. "I had a single three-color frontispiece in my private edition, which was indeed lovely. But I paid for the printing myself so I know the expense. Color will make the book cost more than little rabbits can afford."

Norman smiled. "Little rabbits. How amusing."

Beatrix did not wish to be amusing. "Which brings us to your brothers' second point: they wish to reduce the number of drawings by almost a third. Totally unacceptable."

Norman sat forward. "Miss Potter, let me explain. The idea of reducing the number of drawings was not my brothers' but my own. Here is the scheme. Oh, I am not good at business! If we can reduce the number of drawings to thirty-one precisely, the illustrations for the entire book can be printed on a single sheet of paper, using the, uh what, the three-color process you desire, and at a level of, uh, cost that will keep it within the means of . . . little rabbits. Yes, I think I have that right. Yes."

"Oh," said Beatrix.

"I have given your book a great deal of attention. Truly I have," said Norman with sudden fervor. "I would like it to look colorful on the shelf, so that it stands out from ordinary books."

"My, you have given it thought," said Beatrix. "What other books have you supervised?"

"Personally?" said Norman.

"Yes."

"This will be my first."

"Your first."

"Yes."

"Ah," said Beatrix.

Norman folded his hands over the portfolio. "Miss Potter, F. Warne and Co. was founded by my late father. At his death my elder brothers took charge of the firm. I have recently informed my brothers – and my mother – that I am not content to stay home and play nursemaid, just because I am the youngest son. I wish to have a proper job, and my own place in my family's firm. And they have assigned me you. Does that make things clearer?"

"Very clear," said Beatrix. "In other words, you have no experience whatsoever, but since you've made a nuisance of yourself demanding to be given a chance, your brothers have fobbed you off on me."

Norman's voice took on a sudden and unexpected force. "Miss Potter," he said. "I know only too well what my brothers intended, giving me your 'bunny book,' as they call it. But I find your book enchanting – delightful! If they intended to 'fob me off,' as you say, we shall show them! We are going to give them a children's book to conjure with! In full color!" His enthusiasm carried him right out of his chair.

"But Mr. Warne," Beatrix blurted out, the excitement in the room infecting her, "I do not like the colors in Warne and Co.'s children's books. I will not have those dreadful brown and green washes!"

"Miss Potter," he announced, "I am going to insure that your book will be printed precisely as you wish."

"How will you insure that?"

"Dear lady, I will take you to the printer."

In the corner, Miss Wiggin looked up.

"To the printer?" said Beatrix. "The actual print shop? Mr. Warne, I hardly think . . ."

"I will escort you myself," Norman said, "if you will allow me the honor. The inks will be mixed before your very eyes – precisely as you dictate."

Beatrix felt her hands begin to flutter again. "I'm afraid I could never . . ."

Beatrix stopped herself. Once again a casual moment contained a decision that would determine her life.

"Never?" she said. "Why could I "never"? Of course, I can go. I will go. I'm a grown woman. Miss Wiggin will come along. I see no reason why an artist shouldn't visit her printer."

"We have a cause!" cried Norman. "You . . . and I: a book for children, in beautiful color."

"I warn you," said Beatrix. "I shall also want to be very particular about the copyright. Please be advised that my father is a barrister."

"The copyright? Oh, Miss Potter. Haven't I made myself clear?" said Norman. "Everything shall be as you wish! I am . . . uh, what . . . in every way . . ." He reached out and impulsively took her hand, ". . . at *your* service."

Beatrix looked at Norman's hand holding hers.

A sudden memory flashed through her mind. An image as clear and precise as a Dutch landscape. An estate in the Lake District, the summer of 1882. Beatrix was sixteen, drawing in her sketchbook. Bertram's voice resounded in the summer air. "Beatrix! Come into the garden. The gamekeeper has the puppies!"

Beatrix put down her sketchbook. The gamekeeper? she thought. Another old man who smells bad and won't stop telling stories. Ugh. She trotted off, rounded the corner, entered the garden, and saw . . .

William Heelis, the gamekeeper, throwing a stick and racing full tilt around the lawn with the terrier father of the boxful of puppies that sat on the lawn. William Heelis was twenty-five, young, athletic, wildly handsome, with a shock of fiery red hair!

Beatrix stopped dead. The gamekeeper?

Beatrix's mind snapped back to the present. Why this memory now? she thought. And why of William Heelis, of all people?

Her pause made Norman grow suddenly nervous. He withdrew his hand.

"I shall make all the arrangements," he said, and headed for the door.

Norman realized he was still holding her portfolio. He handed it back to Beatrix, the picture of the rabbit in a blue jacket shining on the cover. As he did so, Norman suddenly saw that the wall behind her head was filled with framed pictures of rabbits – nature studies Beatrix had drawn which her mother found acceptable enough to be displayed.

"Are these your paintings too?" asked Norman, looking from frame to frame.

"Yes."

"You and rabbits!" Norman exclaimed. "Extraordinary!"

Hilda, the housemaid, appeared with Norman's coat. Norman walked out the door, turned back while still walking – and tripped, almost falling on his face.

"Ah, well, no harm done," he said, recovering. "Goodbye, Miss Potter . . . Until . . . well, until very soon!"

Norman continued out to the street, where he turned back to wave and almost tripped again. Beatrix waved back. Against her judgment, she started to laugh.

She kept watching until Norman had disappeared down the street.

She turned to one of the pictures on the wall. "Oh dear, Benjamin," she said. "What have we got ourselves into?"

Chapter Four

Beatrix stood in the hall for a long moment. Benjamin looked down at her from the wall. Was he saying something to her? Even in a drawing, Benjamin always seemed to have an opinion.

Oh dear, she thought. It's true, what Mr. Warne just said! "Beatrix and rabbits!"

She thought back to Benjamin. Benjamin H. Bouncer with his bright inquisitive eyes and face of human expressiveness had been a favorite subject of Beatrix from the day she brought him home, hidden in a paper bag, from a bird shop in London, when she was in her early twenties. She never tired of sketching him, finding his face different every time she looked. The framed picture on the wall that had caught Norman's eye contained no less than six studies of Benjamin's face which Beatrix had arranged on a single page so that people could see how varied was his personality. She took Benjamin with her whenever she traveled, and once, although she had never told this to anyone, Benjamin even appeared to her in a dream, human-sized and wearing a white nightcap.

Beatrix thought back further. This Benjamin Bouncer was not the first Benjamin Bouncer. The first was a rabbit who had been given to Beatrix when she was much younger, before Bertram was born, and the only appearance he ever made in this part of the house was in a hutch during the chaos the Potter family went through every summer when the time came to depart for whatever grand house Rupert had rented.

At this moment, Beatrix had a memory: of the first Benjamin H. Bouncer, locked in a box with air holes, being carried down the stairs by herself at age eleven, while her mother's strident voice resounded through the house.

"Rupert, hurry! Must you be late even for a train? Beatrix! Bertram!" It was the same sentence every year.

It was late May in 1877.

The Potters were well off, wealthy in truth. Rupert's father, Edmund, had rebounded from early failure in business to create the largest and most respected calico printworks in England, perhaps even the world. Mrs. Potter's father, John Leech, was such a successful cotton merchant in Manchester that he built his own boats to import the fibers. The marriage combined these two families, and provided the young couple with a sizable and dependable income. For a very brief moment, it was thought that Rupert might join the family business as his elder brother Crompton had done, but Rupert had no interest in factories and instead chose law. As soon as the couple were married, they moved to London and never looked back.

The Potters, therefore, had ample means to rent a large country house each summer, and to move there for the entire season, avoiding London's heat as all families of quality did. From the time Beatrix was five until she was fifteen, the house of choice was an estate in Scotland called Dalguise House, grand in scale, with vast acreage, a working farm, fields, ponds and glorious woods.

Departures for the summer were a madhouse at 2 Bolton Gardens. Somehow the family was always late. Steamer trunks, hatboxes, suitcases and valises had to be packed and loaded on to the carriage. Something was always forgotten, and the bags always had to be repacked. Cases and cases of equipment were required to support Rupert's new-found hobby of photography. And then there were the children's animals, who could not be left behind. The mice, the jaybird, the white rat and Benjamin Bouncer were all packed in cages or portable hutches for the journey, which they made not in the baggage car but in the train compartment on the laps of the family members.

The race across London to King's Cross Station was always breakneck; the unloading of family, servants and luggage at the street and the subsequent gallop through the crowd to the track always left the family out of breath; and Saunders the coachman always got the luggage on to the train with mere seconds to spare.

On the train the family would sit in exhausted silence. This particular year the only amusement came when the jaybird, whose cage was propped next to Mrs. Potter, suddenly released a large and rather noisy dropping, right beside her face. The children could not avoid laughing, although it was completely inappropriate. Mrs. Potter was too resigned even to wince.

Outside the window, the family watched the landscape change as the train moved from the manicured fields of England into the wildness of Scotland.

Once at Dalguise, life slowed. Mrs. Potter spent her days planning her winter social season and entertaining guests.

Personages like William Gaskell, the theologian, John Millais, the painter, and John Bright, the politician, were among the many family friends who came for extended stays, all of which required extensive planning.

Rupert, freed from any pretense of a career, spent his days photographing everything in sight: his family, his guests, the farm animals, the landscape – and developing the photographs in a darkroom he had set up in a room off the library. The children would often encounter Rupert, every bit the country gentleman in tweed plus-fours and a deerstalker hat, marching happily through the woods with his camera, followed by a servant lumbering along under the weight of the tripod and heavy cases of film. Sometimes the children would pose for Rupert, standing stock-still for the full minute it took to take the picture. Other times they would see Rupert posing the ladies of the estate in "bucolic scenes". Victorians honored the therapeutic value of nature and fresh air, but wanted neither to touch their person. Therefore whenever Mrs. Potter and other lady guests of the estate took long walks and boat rides they went out fully dressed and corseted, covered to the wrists and neck in black fabric, and never without a hat. Rupert posed them sitting like mannequins in a rowing boat, or arrayed like statuary in front of a garden gate.

For the children, summers at Dalguise were idylls. The estate house had, among its many spectacular amenities, a broad terrace at the back that looked down a long lawn to a lake. On this terrace every morning, Nurse McKenzie, whom the children now called by her name, Fiona, would send off the two children in crisp clean play clothes for a day of adventure.

"Mind your frocks now," Fiona said, her thick Scottish burr suddenly made thicker, it seemed to Beatrix, by her return to her homeland. "The woods are filled with fairies and little folk who watch for children who get their clothes dirty. When they find them, they send fairy beasts at night who have sharp teeth and a ready appetite for young flesh."

"Fiona!" said Mrs. Potter.

"Well, it's trooooe!" cried Fiona.

With Fiona's admonishment ringing in their ears, the children would run off. A visitor might come across them anywhere – Beatrix always clean and neat, sketching; Bertram always smudged with dirt and disarrayed.

Dalguise was for the Potter children a true land of Wonders. There were animals to see and draw, both domesticated and wild. One day it was a hedgehog, whom they chased until he disappeared into his hole under an oak tree. Another day it was a huge bullfrog, who sat with sedate dignity on a lily pad in the pond, until they got too close and it took a long genteel leap into the water. They got to know the ducks and geese in the pond so well that they could tell them apart. One white duck who was particularly haughty and stupid and who always made them laugh, they named Jemima. The farm cat cornered a field mouse, and the children held him down until the mouse could escape. One day when Beatrix was sketching, a red fox came trotting down the path straight at her. She had never seen a fox in daylight, and there he was, arrogant and cocksure, with a smile on his face that seemed directed right at her. Was it only Beatrix who noticed that all the animals at Dalguise seemed to have personalities?

One day, Beatrix and Bertram almost got into a fight. Bertram had captured a large and particularly beautiful butterfly in a glass jar, and Beatrix insisted he release it.

"I won't!" said Bertram.

"I won't have you murder an insect just because she's pretty," said Beatrix. "Let her go!" "But I don't have this one!" cried Bertram.

"I don't care!" said Beatrix. She pulled the cap off the bottle, and shook it until the butterfly flew away. "There!" cried Beatrix triumphantly. "Go back to your children! Be free again!"

"She'll die anyway, you know," said Bertram. "I touched her wings." And then he added, "She's an insect, Bee, not a person."

Many days Fiona took the children on outings and picnics, which the children often found terrifying instead of fun. Fiona, still in her twenties, was raised north of Dalguise in the Scottish Highlands, where every wild creature and natural phenomenon had a story to tell. Spider webs glistening with morning dew were fairy ballrooms; a gnarled tree was Prince Charlie's cradle; a wild mountain crag was Bluebeard's nose. For every rock outcropping, fallen tree or cave, there was a goblin, wraith, beast, or tragically abandoned lover whose story Fiona imparted with a relish bordering on the bloodthirsty. The discovery of a squirrel skeleton in the woods gave Beatrix a subject she could draw for hours, and Fiona an opportunity to speculate vividly on how the animal reached its brutal and untimely end.

And so the summer days passed. What with Fiona's endless tales of fairies and monsters, and the children's regular encounters with animals with human characteristics, it was a time of magic. Not surprisingly it also became a time of stories.

Dalguise, beside being a Wonderland, was a working farm, and a vine-covered door in the stone wall that extended out from the side of the main house was the entry to stables, barns, pastures and an enclosed vegetable garden, each of which had its own kind of enchantment. The children were not forbidden to play in the farm areas, but neither were they encouraged, and Mrs. Potter worked hard to ensure that the children felt wary about entering it.

"Beatrix, Bertram," said Mrs. Potter once, as they came upon the three children their age taking turns jumping into a haymow. "Don't play with the gardener's children. Their hands are covered with germs."

The children therefore felt that any foray into the farm area was an adventure tinged with a bit of danger. When they passed through the gate, they could not help but feel that they were trespassing. The vegetable garden, walled in to keep out rodents, was particularly bewitched. Neatly hoed and weeded, it was laid out in perfect rows that seemed to the children like the Minotaur's labyrinth. The children played tag in the garden, being careful never to be so exuberant that they damaged a vegetable. One day when they were passing through rows of tall bean plants, they spied a rabbit hopping between the garden rows. "How did he get in?" Bertram cried out. While the children knew the rabbit should not be in the garden, they also knew the rabbit would have great difficulty getting out. Therefore they resolved to catch him. They sneaked as close as they could, from two sides.

"Come, Peter," said Beatrix, pulling the name from nowhere. "We won't harm you. We want you to meet Benjamin."

The rabbit sensed their presence and bolted. A wild chase followed, over cabbages, around bean fences, under squash plants.

"Go round the tomato plants!" cried Bertram. "I'll fetch a basket and catch him at the cucumbers."

Beatrix did as she was told, and maneuvered the rabbit into a lane of peas. "Don't move, Peter, we're your friends!" she cried, as Bertram pushed through the pea plants, and swung a wicker basket down hard. The rabbit escaped by inches and ran towards Beatrix.

"Catch him, Bee!" cried Bertram.

The rabbit darted for the gate. Beatrix leapt to catch him, but missed and landed instead in a puddle of mud. The rabbit, given a moment's extra time, found his way to the gate and squeezed under it.

Beatrix pulled herself from the puddle. "I guess he'll have a story to tell his mother tonight."

Bertram looked at his mud-covered sister. "So will you," he said.

~

On the terrace, Mr. and Mrs. Potter confronted their bedraggled children. Fiona had presented the children to their parents in order to make their punishment as melodramatic as possible.

49

Fiona considered the young criminals with the solemnity of a Biblical judge. "Nae, I dinna think a thrashing will be necessary," she said in her strongest Scottish accent. "I'll just leave the window in the nursery unlatched tonight. The fairy beasts will take care of the rest."

"No!" cried Bertram.

"Really, Beatrix," said Mrs. Potter, turning to her daughter. "What young man is ever going to marry a girl with a faceful of mud?"

Beatrix was not amused. "I shall never marry, so it doesn't matter."

"Of course you shall marry," said Mrs. Potter. "All girls marry. I did, your grandmother did, even Fiona will, one day."

"Well, I shan't," said Beatrix. "I shall draw."

"Draw?" said Mrs. Potter, sending a look to Mr. Potter. "Then who will love you?"

"My art. My animals. I won't need more love than that. No one does."

Rupert smiled. "Perhaps not at eleven. Let's see if you still feel that way at eighteen."

He looked at his wife. "I drew Mama when we first met. She married me."

Mrs. Potter pursed her lips. "That was in the first flush of courtship, when it's appropriate to be foolish."

Rupert enjoyed making his wife react. This was how his sense of humor operated – although unless one noticed the slight twitch at the corners of his mouth, one would never guess that he had made a joke.

"Fiona," he said, "doesn't mud wash off?"

Bertram's adult voice broke Beatrix's reverie, as she stood in the front hall, letting memories of Benjamin take her back in time.

"I'm off, Bee."

Bertram had come down the stairs carrying a worn leather suitcase. Although it was still morning, Beatrix could see that he was already drunk.

"Quick stop at the club to hit Father for a few bob, then I'm on the road," said Bertram. "But . . . just in case . . ."

"I have ten pounds," said Beatrix. "You can have it." She went into the drawing room to find her purse.

"Did the Messrs Warne come? Did you give them what for?"

"It was another brother, a new one. Quite agreeable, really. I didn't have to argue at all."

She handed Bertram a ten-pound note. "Why do you have to go to Scotland to drink?" she said. "You can get Scotch whiskey around the corner."

Bertram leaned his head against the archway. His eyes became watery. "I'm going to tell you something, Bee. And you must promise never to tell."

"I don't want to hear. Look at you. You can't stand up and it isn't even noon."

"She's . . ." Bertram's voice took on an edge Beatrix had never heard before, a tone somewhere between dreaminess and anger. "She's . . . a farm girl. Very . . . common. Very, very common. Knows naught of rules. She sneaks into my room at night in the dark. I can't even see her, just feel her. She knows a place on the farm piled with nothing

51

but goose down and goose droppings. You haven't lived until . . ."

"Stop it, Bertie. You're drunk and disgusting."

Bertram gave his sister a look. "Are you shocked – or impressed?"

"Why do you do this to yourself?" said Beatrix.

"Perhaps because I have learned that, despite being no scholar and a mediocre artist, I have . . . needs . . . of a sort never mentioned during my brief stay at Oxford."

Beatrix wanted to remain angry with Bertram, but she couldn't sustain it. "I still believe you could be a very good . . ."

"Lawyer? I'm no more suited to the law than Father. Spending every day at the club? Who is he fooling? We live on his inheritance. And Mother's."

Beatrix clutched her portfolio to her breast, as if it were a barrier to Bertram and everything he was saying.

"You're my idol, Bee. Not marrying some stick who will suit mother's social ambitions. Not marrying at all! And now getting yourself published. There's another kind of life out there, I can tell you."

Beatrix looked at her brother, propped against the archway. Thin. Good-looking. Charming smile. Wearing ill-fitting country clothes. Dissipated. Lost.

How did her sweet cherub of a brother grow up to be . . . this?

"Bertram!"

In her mind, she suddenly heard Fiona's voice again.

"Thanks for the wherewithal," said Bertram. "Remember: not a word. I'll write."

And he was gone.

"Bertram! Your turn!" cried Fiona, sending the berobed Beatrix into the nursery. Soon five-year-old angelic Bertram was being scrubbed hard in the bathtub, as Beatrix dried her hair with a towel.

"Ow!" cried Bertram.

"I promised Mrs. Potter I'd get you two children clean, and clean you shall be," said Fiona, scrubbing harder. "At whatever the cost!"

"But that hurts!" cried Bertram.

"Dirt hurts," said Fiona. "See. I can rhyme too."

"And clean is mean," said Beatrix under her breath.

Later, dressed for bed, Beatrix sat in the window seat drawing a picture of the courtyard outside. Fiona brushed her hair. Across the room, Bertram was pinning live butterflies on to a display board.

"Die, you little devils," he said.

"Bertram, ugh!" said Beatrix, without looking up.

Fiona put down the hairbrush. "There. Prince Charming himself couldn't resist such a clean little girl."

"Not when he meets my brother, Vlad the Impaler."

"Got you!" cried Bertram, driving a pin home.

Mrs. Potter's voice sounded from down the stairs. "Fiona!"

Fiona went to the door. "Reprieved, my young reprobates. Bed as soon as I return."

Beatrix continued drawing the scene outside her window.

The nursery, on the top floor as usual, looked out on to the rear courtyard of the estate. Across the cobblestoned court was the stable, connected to the main house by a stone archway. To Beatrix, there was something French and romantic about the scene, like the chateaux she imagined when reading Dumas. It was the cobblestones, she decided.

"Why do people get so unpleasant about marriage?" Beatrix said out loud, more or less to Bertram, who was paying no attention. "Turning yourself into something so a man will choose you. It's horrible! And it has nothing to do with love."

She looked out into the courtyard. In her imagination, she suddenly heard hoof-beats, clattering on the cobbles. The courtyard suddenly became populated with mice dressed like palace guards in *The Three Musketeers*. Through the archway galloped a handsome Cavalier, a terrier, on horseback. He leapt off his horse, dispatching mice left and right with his sword. A red fox, in the robes of Cardinal Richelieu, ran from the house in a fearsome effort to halt the handsome swain. He too was dispatched. The Cavalier climbed the ivy to a bay window at the top of the stable.

"No, no," Beatrix whispered. "Not there. Over here. This window."

The bay window of the stable opened and a lady cat in a silk gown emerged. The Cavalier took her in his arms.

Somehow the end of the story left Beatrix chagrined. She snapped out of her reverie.

"Love is pathetic!" she said out loud. "I'd rather have a pet rabbit."

Fiona returned to the room. "Bedtime!" she announced. Then she stopped, appearing to have a serious thought. "Look now – what about your punishment? Shall I leave the window open, or . . ."

"No!" cried Bertram. "I don't like fairy beasts. I'll stay clean!"

Fiona considered his announcement thoughtfully. "Well," she said, "it *is* a well-known fact that fairy beasts never eat a child when he's tucked in his own bed."

Beatrix and Bertram scrambled into their beds.

Fiona sat down on a rocking chair between them. "The fairies have been in Scotland for hundreds of years, and they have had many adventures. Have I told you about the changeling child?"

"No," said Bertram.

"Yes. Several times," said Beatrix.

"I want to hear it," said Bertram.

"Oh, go ahead, Fiona. Tell him again," said Beatrix. "I'll tell myself a story."

She sank back into her pillow.

Fiona began to rock gently. "Once upon a time, there was a king and queen who had no child . . ."

Beatrix thought back upon the adventures of the day. "Once upon a time . . ." she said to herself, ". . . there were four little rabbits, and their names were . . . Flopsy, Mopsy, Cotton-tail and . . . Peter."

Chapter Five

. . . And their names were Flopsy, Mopsy, Cotton-tail and Peter.

The words had entered Beatrix's head when she was a child, and never left. She remembered them years later when writing a letter to Noel Moore, the son of a former governess. Noel was ill, and it occurred to her that including a little story accompanied by some pictures might cheer him up. The words were back in her head as Beatrix, in her studio, wrote them in perfect calligraphy on a plate to accompany her final drawings for F. Warne and Co. And now the words were on a manuscript in the office of a real publisher, as Beatrix Potter showed her new color paintings to Norman Warne.

. . . "Now, my dears," said old Mrs. Rabbit one morning, "you may go into the fields or down the lane, but don't go into Mr. McGregor's garden. Your father had an accident there; he was put in a pie by Mrs. McGregor . . ."

Without realizing it, each time she had finished a new page, she had found herself picturing Norman Warne's reaction. Would he cry, "Delightful!" and rest his hand on his cheek? Would his face break into that unrestrained smile? Now, in the office, with the entire book in his hand, he reacted with every bit of the delight she had imagined.

He turned the pages slowly, commenting, gasping, marveling, calling clerks over to come and see.

Beatrix stood beside him as he read, suddenly aware of how near she was to him, suddenly aware of the warmth of his tweed suit, suddenly aware of the clean, pleasant scent of witch hazel. She looked up and saw the small stretch of neck between his trimly cut hair and his collar. Mister Warne. She repeated the words to herself. Mister Warne.

> *. . . Peter, who was very naughty, ran straightaway to Mr.*
> *McGregor's garden, and squeezed under the gate! . . .*

A few days later Mr. Warne and Miss Potter, locked in a carriage with Miss Wiggin, were clattering across southeast London to a dull brick building in Swan Street, where a cluttered alley led them to a factory door. Miss Wiggin trotted after them, out of breath. Inside Norman took Beatrix down an aisle of thundering printing presses to one particular machine that had been assigned to her. Norman indicated to the printer that he should begin.

A thrill of excitement came over Beatrix as she watched the inker push his roller over the metal plate. The printer placed a sheet of paper over the matrix, lowered a cover to press the paper down hard, raised the cover, reached out, took the sheet of paper by one corner and carefully drew it back off the plate. He held it up to Beatrix.

"Oh no," said Beatrix.

The blue was deep and heavy. She looked at Norman.

"Too dark," said Norman to the printer. "Try again."

The inker cleaned off the plate with alcohol, added

some white and mixed a new blue tint. Beatrix and Norman waited breathlessly. Miss Wiggin in a nearby chair simply waited. The inker inked the plate again, and the printer put in another sheet.

"Oh dear," said Beatrix. "No!"

"Try again," said Norman to the printer.

Once again the alcohol, the remixing, the rolling, the pressing, and then:

"No!" said Beatrix, disappointed "It's still . . ."

Norman nodded to the printer, whose pleasantness was fading.

. . . but round the end of a cucumber frame, whom should he meet but Mr. McGregor!

The day continued. The inker kept adding white to the blue ink, but each mixture produced only minimal lightening.

"My dear man," said Norman finally, to the printer. "Let us look at the watercolor plate. See. The blue here is ever so much softer and paler."

The inker and the printer looked at the watercolor, huddled together and, with barely suppressed irritation, decided to discard the entire batch of ink. They would start over, they announced, this time with white to which they would add blue. A color proof was held up to Beatrix.

"Much better, but now it's too . . ." said Beatrix. "It's very close," she added, trying to sound positive.

The printer added a dot more indigo. To waste an entire day chasing the whims of a woman! Women should not be allowed in the workplace, he thought. They are too emotional. His thoughts showed on his face. He looked at Norman, who simply nodded firmly that he should proceed. The printer tried again.

. . . Peter was out of breath and trembling with fright, and he had not the least idea which way to go . . .

Norman made the printer try twice more. As Norman grew more and more resolute, Beatrix felt a sudden sensation that she didn't expect. What was it? Comfort, perhaps? Safety? She was being taken care of! Beatrix prided herself on her independence. She rarely asked for help in anything, preferring to solve whatever problem arose by her own wits. With her parents growing older at 2 Bolton Gardens, she had taken to making more and more decisions herself until she now effectively ran the household. It was she who dealt with bricklayers and gardeners and plumbers – and she felt satisfaction when she did. But standing here in the dusty shafts of daylight in a thundering printing house, facing a workman who was growing less friendly with every minute, Beatrix felt a curious relaxation in the presence of a man who, pleasantly and yet with complete firmness, had taken charge. Every now and then Norman looked at her, and Beatrix felt suddenly that she was . . . understood. Had anyone in her life ever understood her?

The exasperated printer held up yet another sheet.

"Yes," said Beatrix.

"Well done!" said Norman to the man. There was a sigh of relief all around. "Excellent work, sir," said Norman, with such sincerity that the printer forgot that he was angry. Norman smiled again. "Now let's see to the reds."

. . . Mr. McGregor caught sight of him at the corner, but Peter did not care. He slipped underneath the gate, and was safe at last in the wood outside . . .

Later that week, Beatrix and Norman stood at the printing press as page after page rolled out of the machine to be lifted on a wooden palette, flipped over in the air, and deposited in a box at the back. There in the box it was: the entirety of her book, printed on two sides of a single sheet, in soft luxurious colors. Beatrix and Norman beamed. Miss Wiggin watched from a distance, bored to the point of distraction.

. . . I am sorry to say that Peter was not very well during the evening. His mother put him to bed, and made some camomile tea; and she gave a dose of it to Peter! "One table-spoonful to be taken at bed-time." . . . But Flopsy, Mopsy, and Cotton-tail had bread and milk and blackberries for supper.

Beatrix and Norman looked at this last page of the book, which was now bound together in a mock-up, and then they leafed backwards to the front. There the images were: McGregor almost catching Peter with a garden sieve, Peter getting his coat trapped by the buttons in a gooseberry net, Peter losing his shoes among the potatoes. Finally there was the title page: *The Tale of Peter Rabbit*, by Beatrix Potter.

Beatrix weighed the finished book in her hand. Tears came to her eyes. She became embarrassed and wiped the tears away, looked up at Norman and their eyes met.

It was only for an instant, but it seemed for Beatrix to be

an eternity, so long that she had to look away.

"Miss Potter," said Norman, "I wonder if . . . I don't want to be, um . . . my family . . . the other Warnes . . . would greatly like to . . ."

~

It was not long after that a footman arrived at the Potter house with an invitation. Would Miss Beatrix Potter do Mrs. Frederick Warne the honor of visiting No. 8 Bedford Square for tea on Thursday next?

The Warne family's house in Bedford Square was large and imposing, not unlike the house at 2 Bolton Gardens, although the Potter house was much newer. Norman's mother, in her seventies and in a wheelchair, and his unmarried sister, Millie, who was Beatrix's age, were waiting for them in the drawing room when Beatrix and Norman arrived. Miss Wiggin was ushered aside into the servants' quarters by a Warne maid.

"Mother dear," said Norman, "this is Miss Potter."

Mrs. Warne liked to play the frail elderly lady, and dressed the part, lace at the neck and wrist, hair pulled back under a snood, small spectacles. It was all pretense. Mrs. Warne was sharp as a tack, missed nothing, and aside from problems with her knees that limited her walking, was in perfect health.

"At last," she said, " we poor forgotten folk in Bedford Square get to share some of Norman's excitement."

Beatrix offered her hand. "Mrs. Warne, how kind of you to invite me."

"Kind?" said Mrs. Warne, with an actressy grandeur. "It

was the desperate act of a mother who was beginning to forget what her son looked like."

Norman ignored the tone. "And this, Miss Potter, is Millie."

Amelia Warne, bounding in from the far doorway, took Beatrix by surprise. She was outgoing, warm, full of unexpected exuberance – unlike the rest of the Warne family, and, truth to tell, unlike most of the women Beatrix had ever met. Millie was wearing a shirtwaister blouse in cream-colored stripes, with a necktie and jacket, although there was nothing mannish about her. Millie was a little overweight, and her look, while fashionable, was not entirely pulled together.

"Norman allowed us a peek at Peter Rabbit, Miss Potter," said Millie. "I hope you don't mind. I became so curious, after all his talking, I simply had to see for myself. We found it absolutely charming."

Mrs. Warne stretched her hand toward a bell on the table which was just out of her reach. "I'll ring for tea, Mother," said Millie, and did so, without breaking stride.

". . . So we wheedled, cajoled, absolutely insisted, that Norman bring you round for tea. I have decided that you and I are going to be friends."

"Have you?" said Beatrix.

Millie leaned forward, her eyes flicking to her mother to make sure she was listening. "Norman tells me you are unmarried, as I am. And not unhappy about it! I can't tell you how that pleases me."

Mrs. Warne harrumphed. "Oh, Millie. Why can't you talk about the weather, like other girls?"

Millie chattered on. "All the other unmarried daughters

in our circle – and there seem to be *hundreds* – are so gloomy it puts me right out of sorts to be with them. But you are doing something! You don't sit around all day gossiping and tatting and unaccountably bursting into tears. You have written a book! I warn you, I am prepared to like you very much."

"In that case," said Beatrix, "I shall have to like you too, Miss Warne."

"Call me Millie, please. And I'm afraid that's going to have to be the last of "Miss Potter" too."

"Absolutely. Beatrix, by all means."

A maid appeared with a tray.

"Thank goodness, the tea," said Mrs. Warne. "I was beginning to feel ill from all this bonhomie."

Millie leapt out of her chair. "Let's have tea in the garden, Mother. It's too beautiful a day – in *every* way – not to share it with the flowers."

Millie threw open the French doors at the back of the parlor. Sunlight flooded the room. Behind the house was a flagstone terrace surrounded by a perfect English garden. Tea roses, foxgloves, phlox and agapanthus spilled over themselves, in contained disorder. Borders of pansies and forget-me-nots lapped the stone floor, and four giant hydrangea bushes provided a backdrop of massive blue blossoms.

"Bring Mother, Norman," said Millie. "See, Mother, I do notice the weather."

Norman wheeled Mrs. Warne's chair around the cherub fountain in the entry, and the tea party was moved outdoors.

The tea was impressive. There were cucumber finger

sandwiches, scones, toast rounds and teacakes, pots of fresh crème fraiche. Millie took eating seriously, buttering the scones and making real use of several pots of jam.

"This is my garden, really," said Millie between bites. "You draw, Beatrix. Gardening is my art. Mother disapproves, but every day I simply put on my old muslin dress, come out into the garden and dig. I can't help myself. I love flowers so."

"And you have the hands of a greengrocer," sniffed Mrs. Warne. "Thank heavens Norman is here during the day to read to me. If I had to depend on you for companionship, I should expire of loneliness."

"Mother's taste, in books and I'm afraid in life," said Norman, "runs to the, um, melodramatic."

"Nonsense," said Mrs. Warne. "I like good English biographies, and you know it. I loathe silly romances, such as the ones your brothers publish."

"My brothers and I, Mother," said Norman. "I'm part of the firm now."

"A sweet-natured boy like you does not need to work," said Mrs. Warne. "Your brothers provide quite well for all of us. And I need your smile here. But then no one listens to a crotchety old lady in a wheelchair."

"Indeed they don't, Mother," said Norman, affably.

Beatrix felt compelled to enter the conversation. "I understand how one can become obsessed with a garden. That's how I feel about painting. When I see a beautiful object, I am overcome by a desire to copy it. Sometimes I ask myself, "Why can't you be content to *look* at it?" But I cannot rest. I must draw it. And when I'm out of sorts, or a bad time comes over me, the need is stronger than ever.

Last summer, I was in the farmyard drawing something that looked quite lovely in the sun, and I suddenly realized I was drawing the pig's swill bucket. I stopped short, and the laugh I enjoyed quite brought me round."

There was a moment's silence. "I'm feeling a bit of a chill," said Mrs. Warne. "Norman, can you take me inside?"

"Of course, Mother." He went to her chair.

"It was delightful meeting you, Miss Potter," said Mrs. Warne, as Norman wheeled her away. "Do stay longer and enjoy the sun."

A perfectly mannered English tea, in a sublime English garden – who would have noticed that a battle had been raging. Millie piped up with a parting salvo, loudly, for her mother's benefit.

"Mother may not have caught your point, Beatrix. You have something you love. Your art. You don't need anything else."

Mrs. Warne turned to Norman as he wheeled her out. "Did she say she likes to draw swill buckets?"

"Yes, she did, Mother," said Norman. "Indeed she did."

Chapter Six

It was not long after that Beatrix's mother burst into the day room where Beatrix was doing the household accounts, dragging in tow their trembling laundress, Mary. Mary was terrified of Mrs. Potter, terrified of the garment she held in her hand, terrified of simply being above stairs.

"Beatrix, what is this stain on your dress?"

Beatrix looked up from the writing desk.

"Mary says it won't wash out and she's tried everything. She was too afraid to tell you, but Hilda brought her to me."

Beatrix regarded the dress blandly. "It's ink, Mother."

"*Ink?*"

"I must have brushed against something at the printer's," said Beatrix. "I'm terribly sorry, Mary, for causing you extra work."

Mrs. Potter turned to the laundress. "Take the dress away, Mary, and give it to the poor."

Mary, thrilled to be dismissed, ran out of the room and back downstairs.

Mrs. Potter turned back to Beatrix. "I don't think your response shows a very high regard for your father's money," she said.

Beatrix returned to her ledger book. "Perhaps someday my book will sell enough so that I can buy my own clothes.

I'm too old to be living off the generosity of my father."

"You're too old to be spending so much time in the company of a man who takes you to printers. Your father does not approve and neither do I."

"Mr. Warne is publishing my book, Mother," said Beatrix without looking up.

"Oh, that book!" cried Mrs. Potter. "I can hardly wait till it's out and forgotten. I don't understand you, Beatrix. Your father and I have introduced you to so many suitable young men of your class."

"Have you indeed, Mother?"

"Yes. In this very house. In this very room. Young men of fortune and good family. But you told us to stop, and we love you and so we did. Or have you forgotten our efforts there as well?"

"Forgotten? Mother, hardly."

If Mrs. Potter had been able to enter her daughter's mind, which she never ever attempted to do, she would have known that an image once impressed there never left, but remained fixed like one of her father's photographs. At the mention of suitors, images flicked into Beatrix's brain, bright and real and vivid. Forget her "menagerie of suitors"? Beatrix glanced into the drawing room and she could see them, in all their glorious horror, as if they were still just a few feet away.

There was tea with Lady Stokely, an extravagantly dressed woman of ostentatious breeding and substantial means who came to the house accompanied by her nitwit of a son, Lionel. Lionel had curly white-blond hair and a pasty face, and to Beatrix looked for all the world like an over-dressed sheep.

"Lionel is a particular favorite of his great uncle, the Earl, whom we visit every summer at Stokely Court," bleated Lady Stokely in a nasal voice.

Eighteen-year-old Beatrix, sitting primly with hands folded in her lap, looked at Lionel grazing on a finger sandwich, and from her perspective, Lionel suddenly *was* a sheep, a real sheep in an ill-fitting collar and an expensive suit. Beatrix laughed to herself. Perfect! she thought.

Beatrix blinked again and there was another tea. A prune-faced matron named Mrs. Arthur Haddon-Bell sat with her burly clod of a son, Harry, who had just shoved the better part of a gooseberry muffin in his mouth.

Mrs. Haddon-Bell had a voice of porcine orotundity. "Harry's great-grandfather went to Sandhurst, Harry's grandfather went to Sandhurst, Harry's father went to Sandhurst, and so Harry went to Sandhurst. It's assumed that the Haddon-Bells will be military men."

Beatrix looked at Harry, cheeks stuffed with food, his pug nose showing more nostril than one would expect of a human, and Harry suddenly *was* a pig, pink and hairless, squeezed into a too-small uniform that dripped military braid. Beatrix laughed again, and blinked him away.

Oh, there were so many teas! In this very room, as her mother said. So many mothers, so many . . . odd young men. Her "menagerie of suitors," she came to call them. In some people's memory they might have blended together. In Beatrix's mind, each remained unique and distinct. But there was one in particular . . .

Lady Clifford, bone-thin and high browed, watched as her snob of a son, Ashton, was handed Beatrix's

68

sketchbook. Much to Beatrix's chagrin, Mrs. Potter had decided that Beatrix's artistic leanings might, with the Cliffords, enhance her desirability.

"Aren't they lovely drawings, Ashton?" brayed Lady Clifford. "Isn't Beatrix clever?"

Ashton leafed through the book with no interest whatsoever. "Grandfather commissions paintings of all his horses. There's one of a bay hunter I rode in Norfolk, shown in the very silks I wore, that's particularly eye-catching. And I'm told he pays a pretty penny for them." He closed the book and handed it back to Beatrix. "You should take up horse portraits, Miss Potter."

Horse portraits! Oh, yes, thought Beatrix. Exactly! And in her mind Ashton became a grandly framed, insufferably vain, racehorse, dressed in hunting pinks. It was not in fact such a huge change, since Ashton Clifford's face was decidedly horsey to begin with.

"More tea?" said Mrs. Potter, realizing that the interview was careening off course. She rang a small bell.

Ashton leaned forward. "Do you hunt, Miss Potter?"

"Do you mean fox hunt?" said Beatrix.

"I mean any kind of hunting," said Ashton. "Grouse. Deer. Hedgehogs. Pigeons."

Lady Clifford beamed. "Ashton's a crack shot," she said.

Ashton was now unstoppable. "Father and I and the gamekeeper often go out in the morning and shoot breakfast," he said.

"You must come for a weekend, Beatrix," said Lady Clifford. "You'll have such fun, the two of you."

Images of a country weekend flashed through Beatrix's

mind. Dead birds plunging from the sky. Assassinated deer buckling under their weight and falling down dead. Corpses of rabbits and . . .

Into the room came Lydia, a country girl who had been hired by the Potters as a maid-in-training because she also had possible skills as a cook. Lydia's thick North Country accent did her in after several months, but tea with the Cliffords occurred during her short employment, and the image of Lydia, dressed uncomfortably in maid's uniform and cap, offering a tray of hot tarts to Ashton Clifford, remained burned in Beatrix's mind. Except, of course, in her mind, Lydia was a large white country cat.

Ashton was in full narrative when Lydia appeared. "Mother says – Thank you –" He took a tart from the tray. "Mother says I have a particularly steady eye, which I do, but the real secret I've found is the gun. You have to make sure your man cleans it impeccably. The proper oil. The proper cloth." He took a bite of the tart. "If it's not right, you make him do it again. Once when I was taking bead on a magpie, just as I pulled the trigger, I sensed grit in the barrel. And of course I missed. I made my man clean the gun again right on the spot. This is delicious!"

"Thank you, sir," purred the white cat, bobbing as she had been told. "It's my speciality."

"Ah! And what is it?" said Ashton, popping the remainder of the tart in his mouth.

"It's mouse pie," said the cat.

Ashton gagged. Lady Clifford screamed and spilled her tea on her lap. Mrs. Potter choked.

Of course, none of this happened. Ashton ate his tart, chattering away. Lady Clifford watched him adoringly.

Lydia, plump and hopeless, cleared plates.

But Beatrix, demure and unimpressive, sat suppressing an inner smile. She had had her revenge.

All these images flew through Beatrix's brain in no more than a few seconds. She blinked, to put them away. Mrs. Potter was still standing in the doorway.

"You could have chosen to marry," said Mrs. Potter. "You could have your own house, your own family, your own clothes."

Hilda the maid appeared behind her. "Mr. Warne is at the door, ma'am."

Beatrix put down her pen. "Mr. Warne? He's not expected."

Mrs. Potter grumbled. "Unannounced. How perfect."

Beatrix went to the front door where Norman stood, hat in hand, breathless.

"I'm sorry to come by unannounced, dear lady," he said, "but do you think it possible you can come with me right now?"

"Where? What is it?" said Beatrix.

"It's a surprise," said Norman. "I have my carriage here." And he added, "You won't be disappointed."

Beatrix thought for a moment. Nothing in her life happened without planning and preparation. But then, nothing about knowing Norman was expected. "Well . . . yes, I suppose I can. I'll get my coat." Beatrix turned to the maid. "Hilda, fetch Miss Wiggin. Tell her we're going out."

Mrs. Potter had passed them and was now on her way upstairs. "Where is she going?" she said to Hilda, as she reached the landing.

"I don't know where, Mother!" said Beatrix loudly, so her mother could hear. "It's a secret!"

"And when will she return?" Mrs. Potter asked Hilda.

"Maybe never, Mother!"

Chapter Seven

Half an hour later, Norman's carriage clattered down Charing Cross Road and came to a stop at Cecil Court, an arcade of shops not far from the Warne and Co. offices in Covent Garden. Beatrix and Norman got out, followed by a very disgruntled Miss Wiggin.

"Come," said Norman. "No need to hurry, of course, but . . . Oh, let's hurry."

Norman took Beatrix's arm and led her down the walk to a shop with a large book hanging over the door. There, in the window of Wilkins Booksellers, propped up among a dozen other books, was a copy of *The Tale of Peter Rabbit* by Beatrix Potter.

Norman watched Beatrix's face.

"It's for sale," he said.

"Oh my!" said Beatrix. "*Oh my!*"

"See, inside, on the table there. The stack of books. They're all *Peter Rabbit.*"

"Oh my, oh my!" said Beatrix.

"Wait. Look there," said Norman.

Through the window, they could see the shopkeeper and several customers. One well-dressed matron in a picture hat passed the table where the book was displayed. She stopped. She picked up the book!

Beatrix let out a small cry. Norman shouted, "Ah!" Instantly embarrassed, they ducked backwards out of sight. Just as quickly their heads reappeared, as they looked back inside.

The well-dressed woman put the book back on the table.

"Oh dear," said Beatrix.

"Drat," said Norman.

A second woman had been watching the first, and now, out of curiosity, went to the table and picked up *The Tale of Peter Rabbit* herself. She leafed through it. She smiled. Something in the book had amused her!

Outside the window, Beatrix and Norman bit their lips at the tension.

The second woman put the book down and moved on.

Disaster! Beatrix looked at Norman in dismay.

"Wait," said Norman. "Look."

The second woman returned to the book table, thought a moment, picked up a copy of *Peter Rabbit* and took it to the counter. She opened her purse. She took out money. She bought the book!

Outside, Beatrix and Norman hopped around giddily, laughing like children. Miss Wiggin, standing at a distance, tried to pretend she didn't know them.

Beatrix and Norman looked back into the shop. The first woman, having watched the second pay for the book, returned to the table, picked up a copy for herself – and brought it to the counter.

Brilliant! Extraordinary! Beatrix let out a whoop. Norman laughed out loud. They both put their hands to their mouths to regain decorum – and then unable to keep control, exploded into laughter again. Miss Wiggin looked up at the sky, asking for a miracle.

Beatrix and Norman returned to the window to spy some more.

~

Some time later, Beatrix and Norman were having tea and scones in a small pavilion beside the lake in Kensington Gardens. Sunlight shimmered on the water. A haze of pink flowers colored the hedges. Children were rolling hoops and launching sailing boats. Miss Wiggin sat at a nearby table by herself.

Norman jotted in a small notebook. "Two sold during the hour we were at the bookseller. Let's say eight during the whole day. That would amount to forty during the week."

"Forty!" cried Beatrix. "I can't breathe."

"Which means," Norman continued, "one hundred and sixty in a month, and — wait a minute, twelve times sixteen — one eighty-two: eighteen hundred and twenty in a year."

"Gracious!" said Beatrix. "My private edition was two hundred and fifty. I thought that was enormous."

"And that was only one shop," Norman said, closing his notebook. "My dear Miss Potter, you are about to become a very wealthy young author."

Beatrix felt suddenly at a loss. "Hardly young. And as for wealthy, my father already has sufficient means. But suppose . . ." She stopped. "My, what a thought."

Her mind flashed with a set of startling new images: herself, sweeping into a store like some kind of majestic emu, handbag under her feathered wing; boarding a steamship attended by a retinue of liveried rabbits;

sitting in a box at the opera beside bejeweled peacocks. She shook the images away.

"What would it mean to have my own money?" she said out loud. "I could have . . . my own life. My! What things might I do?"

A different thought elbowed its way into her mind. An image of a duck in a bonnet and shawl. She had drawn it years ago. Why remember it now?

And with it came yet another thought.

"What's the matter?" said Norman.

"The matter?" said Beatrix.

"A cloud just passed across your face."

Beatrix collected herself. "I am an unmarried woman who recently decided she should get out of her house and join the world. You have been most generous with your time and have shown me many wonders I would never have seen. Printing houses!" She put her hands in her lap. "I shall miss your company."

Norman looked surprised. "Are you losing my company?"

"I suddenly had the thought that . . . the book is out. Our association is coming to an end."

There was a pause. A wisp of breeze passed, carrying with it the distant sound of children laughing at the lake.

Norman leaned forward, unsure of how to say what he knew he wanted to say. "Miss Potter, I . . ." He reached for her hand, across the table.

Beatrix became aware of Miss Wiggin at the adjoining table, watching them. Beatrix moved her hand, without letting Norman's hand touch it.

"I was hoping . . ." Norman went on, after a second's

pause, "that you might have more stories."

"Strange," said Beatrix. "I was just thinking of one I had almost forgotten, about a duck. A very stupid duck."

"Based on someone you know?"

"Based on myself, I think," said Beatrix. "It's a story I told someone once."

Norman looked at Beatrix, sitting primly, her hands now back in her lap, her eyes distant, filled with a story he could not see. Something changed in him, right then. For the first time that he could remember, he felt able to talk. And he had so many things to say.

"Miss Potter, when my mother became ill, it was simply assumed that I, being the youngest, would stay at home and be her companion. It's only been in the last year that I asked to join my brothers in the firm. I too felt that I should . . . join the world, as you say. I don't have many friends, as of course you have."

"Me?" said Beatrix. "Unless you count my animals and my drawings, I have none. I wasn't like most young ladies I knew. I preferred my brother, and painting, and being alone to the . . ." she searched for the right word, ". . . exhaustion . . . of having friends."

She paused. Another image came into her head, the one that always seemed to appear whenever she was with Norman.

"I did have one friend," she said carefully.

"Yes?"

"My family used to summer in the Lake District," said Beatrix. "A man there opened my eyes. When I was sixteen." The words came carefully. Beatrix realized she was saying something she had never shared with anyone.

Norman felt suddenly nervous. "A man?"

"Yes," said Beatrix. "He taught me to see things, to . . . love things. Yes, I think love is the accurate word. I did quite love him."

Norman's face fell. "I see. How nice."

"He was the gamekeeper on the estate Father had rented for us."

Norman was not happy with where this story was going. "The gamekeeper?"

"Yes," said Beatrix. "I met him the year he was to be married."

Norman felt a wave of relief. "To be married!" he said.

Beatrix grew thoughtful. "Of course I didn't know that then. I was, well, sixteen."

~

It was 1882. Beatrix, aged sixteen, was sketching a gnarled log that she had found beside a pathway in which, remarkably, a seed had rooted and was now trying to grow into some kind of plant. She heard a noise and looked up. Down the path strode a young man with red hair, throwing a stick ahead of him for his dog.

Beatrix felt a flush of . . . oh dear, what was it? . . . excitement, embarrassment, nervousness? Perhaps all of them. She had never before felt such a response simply to seeing someone in the distance.

"Good morning, Mr. Heelis," she called.

William Heelis was rough-hewn and full of energy, the sort of man who never strolls but strides full out. He had a shock of wild red hair. Fox red. Beatrix attempted a cool demeanor, which is not easy when one's heart is audibly thumping.

"Good day to you, Miss Beatrix!" Mr. Heelis called out. "And what a day Mother Nature has made for us! What are you about today?"

Beatrix held up her sketchbook. "I am collecting Wonders. And putting them down in my book."

"Wonders, are they?" said Mr. Heelis, looking at the drawing of the gnarly log. "And very wonderful indeed."

She turned back some pages and showed him other drawings: mushrooms, a wolf's skull, a lizard and countless odd-shaped flowers and leaves.

"You have such talent!" said William Heelis. "I have none I fear, but I do like pictures."

"Do you?" said Beatrix, helpless to think of anything else to say.

"Yes. I visited an art museum once. In London. Paintings from France they were. Just pictures of shoes and trees and bowls of fruit and the like. Never forgot them."

"Whenever I find unusual things, I like to draw them," said Beatrix. "I call them Wonders."

"You love nature, Miss Beatrix. Good for you. I don't suppose many young ladies do." Mr. Heelis took out a pocket watch. "I'm on my way to . . . But as you have an interest in such things, I think I know a Wonder you may not have seen before. Do you have a little time? I could show you. It's a bit of a walk."

"I . . ." said Beatrix helplessly. "I don't think . . ."

Mr. Heelis smiled. "I'll see if Fiona can accompany us," he said.

Shortly thereafter, Mr. Heelis was striding down a cart

road, Beatrix, Fiona and the dog Pip racing to keep up. Suddenly Mr. Heelis started to sing, full out – a folk song about the beauty of England. Mr. Heelis had a voice so strong that his words echoed back from the nearby hills. It seemed to fill the entire valley. They crested a hill, and saw before them a landscape of natural perfection.

Mr. Heelis interrupted his song and swept his arm expansively. "Look, Miss Beatrix. It's a miracle, isn't it? This English countryside. Lush and ripe. Bursting with bounties, fruit, flowers. Look at that cherry tree. Stare at it. Don't you feel its power? Doesn't it seem to explode with energy?"

This perhaps was not the wisest way to talk to an impressionable girl with a swooning crush on you. But no one, not Mr. Heelis, not Fiona, seemed to have noticed the turmoil churning inside this cloistered adolescent.

Beatrix gasped for breath and looked up at Mr. Heelis. His head blocked the sun, throwing his face into complete shadow. All she could see was his shaggy halo of red hair.

"It does. Yes, I can see it," she said desperately.

Mr. Heelis turned into the light. "Is it any wonder those French artists I saw in London want to paint such things, catching – what is it they call 'em – the "impressions" of the light?"

"Yes indeed," said Beatrix. "It is very . . . um . . . thrilling."

"And in danger, miss. People can't afford to keep these beautiful estates intact, so they break them up. Once that happens, they will never be restored. People round here are trying to create a land trust, wherein instead of an estate being sold, it can be donated to public ownership, to preserve the countryside. How to do it legal-wise, that's the question. They intend to enlist summer residents in the cause. Like your parents. And you."

Beatrix stammered. "Me? But I'm only . . ."

"Yes, I know," said Mr. Heelis. "But these affairs take time, and you won't be a child for long." He looked at her. "No, not long at all." He regarded her for a moment. "But this is not the Wonder I had in mind," he said. "Come with me now. I hope it hasn't disappeared. Wonders have a habit of going scarcely they've arrived. Come, Pip."

He left the cart road and followed a path downhill. It led them lower and lower through trees and moss-covered groves towards a depression in the valley. Once, in their descent, they had to navigate a steep slope. Beatrix slipped on the leaf-strewn earth and Mr. Heelis's big hand grabbed her arm to prevent a fall.

"Pardon, miss."

Beatrix felt the strength of his arm, and once again became breathless. "No. Really. It's perfectly . . ."

"I can see you're out of breath," said Mr. Heelis. "Perhaps a short rest?"

"No. No, thank you," gasped Beatrix.

They entered a clearing. Beatrix felt a desperate need to make conversation. But what was she to say?

"Mr. Heelis, I've never asked: how is it you came to be gamekeeper on an estate, when you're so young?"

"My father was the gamekeeper. He contracted the tuberculosis when I was eighteen, and died of it. The owner always liked me for reasons known only to him. Said he saw things in me even I didn't see. And so the job became mine."

"You're lucky," she said. Oh no! she thought instantly. How could I say that! I must be the clumsiest child!

"Not your father dying of course," she said, helplessly. She gestured out, "I mean, this. Living in such a beautiful place."

"To tell the truth, day to day, it disappears for me, miss. But seeing it through your eyes makes me mindful of what I'm giving up."

"You're leaving?"

"Oh, I've left. I'm just here to help out for the summer. Foolish notion, perhaps, but, involving myself in all the talk about the land trust, I felt a hankering to study law. In Manchester. To better myself."

"How could you leave all this for a dirty city?"

"It doesn't feel like my doing, miss," said Mr. Heelis. "A larger force at work perhaps. Life has a habit of leading you on if you listen to it, and you must follow where it goes, willy-nilly."

They had come to a cleft in a rock forming the boundary of a dark copse. "We're here," said Mr. Heelis. He gestured into the darkness. "The Wonder I spoke of is through here – that is, if you're game. I warn you, it gets a little dangerous. Do you think you are prepared for a bit of danger?"

"Well, I suppose . . ." stammered Beatrix. "Yes, I'll go." She turned to her chaperone. "Fiona?"

"Nae, I'll stay right here. No deeper for me," said Fiona. "I dinna like the smell in the air. This is a haunted place. I fear the creatures that live here. I feel their presence. They're very near. And I . . ."

"Fiona, please!" cried Beatrix.

"I'll go first," said Mr. Heelis. He pushed through the

underbrush, and he and Pip disappeared inside the copse.

Beatrix swallowed hard and followed him.

Inside the copse, Beatrix could see very little. "This way," said Mr. Heelis. His hand appeared through the foliage, extended out to her. Beatrix saw that his arm had soft red hair on it.

"You give me courage, Mr. Heelis," Beatrix said. She took his hand and let him draw her into the darkness.

Beyond the dark was a pond. Mr. Heelis led Beatrix and Pip into an overgrown, damp and mossy grove, a silent and magical world with filmy strands of greenery hanging from the branches overhead. The foul smell of decay permeated the air.

Beatrix gasped at the odor. "Ohh! Urghhh!"

"Beg pardon, Miss Beatrix," said Mr. Heelis. "It stinks to high heaven, I know, but I think that's why the Wonder is here. We're getting close."

He ducked under a tree branch, made his way to a rotting log, squatted down and looked. "They're still here. Come."

Beatrix walked gingerly to join him. At the base of the log, extraordinary formations of fungi thrust up out of the wood rot. Some were red and bulbous, some were concave and alluring. Beatrix winced at their foul smell, and — what was it that was so . . . startling about their shapes?

"Horrible!" she exclaimed. "And astonishing. They look as if they have escaped from some ancient world."

"And they disappear without trace after a few days," said Mr. Heelis. "They aren't pretty, but they qualify as a Wonder in my book."

Mr. Heelis looked at the fungi and suddenly saw them through Beatrix's eyes. They weren't mere oddities. They looked . . . anatomical. Mr. Heelis suddenly felt he had made a mistake bringing young Miss Potter here. These particular Wonders were not at all fit for a young girl.

"I'd happily sit here for hours and draw it if the smell were more pleasant," said Beatrix.

"And I'd stay with you if I wasn't running late," said Mr. Heelis, happy for the excuse. "Time to go I'm afraid."

They retraced their path out of the mystic grove.

Released at last, Fiona could not stop talking. "Foul, hateful place. The smell of slaughter was everywhere. It was in such a glen that the great She-Wolf lived. She kidnapped infants from their cradles and fed them to her sucklings . . ."

"Fiona, please!" cried Beatrix. "Can we do without your stories, for once?"

"If you don't like mine, tell one of your own," said Fiona. "It's a pagan grove, and stories are our only defense. Oh, I fear for my dreams tonight!"

"You make up stories, Miss Beatrix?" asked Mr. Heelis. They had reached the steep slope which Beatrix and Fiona were going to need help climbing. "Perhaps we should all take a short rest up top, and you can tell us one." He climbed halfway, reached out his hand, first to Beatrix and then Fiona, and pulled them up the hill.

"I do have one story," Beatrix said, uncertainly, as they arrived at a flat rock at the top. "I'm not sure I remember all of it, but . . . it's been in my head all day."

"What's it about, then? Is it a . . ."

"Duck!" blurted out Beatrix.

Thinking he was being warned, Mr. Heelis jumped back and hit his head on a branch. "Ow!"

"Oh no! I'm sorry," said Beatrix. She raised her hand to do something, but . . . what? Comfort his bruised head? Her hand hovered uselessly, then fell back to her side. "The story . . . is *about* a duck. Jemima Puddle-duck was her name, and . . ." she let out an audible sigh, ". . . and a stupider duck the world has never seen!" Beatrix looked around, feeling miserable and gauche. Her eye lit on the canvas bag she had given to Fiona. "If you like, I'll draw her for you." She leapt to the bag, opened her sketchbook, took out a charcoal pencil, and sat down.

The moment she began drawing, she felt at ease again.

"See. Here she is." With just a few quick lines, the character began to take shape. "Now, one fine spring afternoon, Jemima flew off to find a place to lay her eggs." She spoke with a sudden fierce intensity, not taking her eyes off the paper. "Jemima was wearing . . ." Her pencil flicked across the page and the details appeared, ". . . a shawl and a poke bonnet."

"Like you," said Mr. Heelis.

"Quite," said Beatrix. She looked up at Mr. Heelis for just an instant, then returned to the page. "When she landed, Jemima was startled to find . . . an elegantly dressed gentleman in a green tweed coat, reading a newspaper. He had black prick ears. And red hair. Fox-red hair."

"Like mine," said Mr. Heelis.

"As a matter of fact, yes," said Beatrix. "But with very sharp teeth."

Mr. Heelis bared his teeth playfully.

"Precisely," said Beatrix. "Jemima told the gentleman

her quest, and the gentleman said he had a shed behind his house that would be perfect for laying eggs. He took her to see it. Jemima was surprised that the shed had *so many feathers* in it, but then, as I told you, she was a very stupid duck."

Mr. Heelis laughed out loud. He looked over at Beatrix, amazement on his face. "Miss Beatrix, I had no idea . . ." He groped for the right word. "Your story is . . . funny."

"Not in any way. It's very serious," Beatrix said soberly, stripping the smile from her face. Inside, however, she felt the sudden pleasurable sensation of having made a connection with Mr. Heelis. He had gotten the joke.

"Shall I go on?"

"Please."

"Jemima Puddle-duck made her nest, produced nine eggs and began to sit on them." Beatrix lowered her voice to sound masculine. "'Madam, I beg you,' said the bushy-tailed gentleman . . . Did I tell you he had a bushy tail?"

"No, you didn't," said Mr. Heelis, laughing again.

"Well, he did," said Beatrix, straight-faced. "'Madam,' said the gentleman, 'before you commence your tedious sitting, let us have a dinner party, just ourselves. Bring some herbs from the garden — sage and thyme, mint and two onions, and some parsley. I'll provide the rest. We'll have a roast and omelets. You do like omelets, don't you?' Jemima was such a simpleton, even the mention of omelets didn't make her suspicious."

Mr. Heelis laughed so hard that he rolled on to his back. Making Mr. Heelis laugh made Beatrix feel suddenly grown up.

"Jemima left her nine fat eggs and returned to the farm.

She went round the garden, gathering a quantity of what were in fact all the herbs required for stuffing roast duck." Mr. Heelis let out a whoop of laughter. "Now it happened that on the farm there was a collie." Beatrix assumed a heroic dog voice. "'Where are you going with all those herbs?' the dog asked, and Jemima told him about the polite gentleman with the bushy red hair. The collie asked her the exact location of the shed. When Jemima arrived at the shed, she heard all manner of barks and yelps from inside. The collie opened the door. The gentleman was gone and was never seen again – Did I tell you the collie had brought along two fox hounds?"

"No, but I might've guessed! So, your story even has a happy ending," laughed Mr. Heelis.

"Not at all," said Beatrix soberly. "This story has an *unhappy* ending. I'm afraid the fox hounds were so excited, they ran into the shed and ate all the eggs. Jemima had to lay more. And she never understood what had happened to her."

She showed Mr. Heelis her sketchpad. She now had an exquisite finished drawing of Jemima carrying an egg basket. Mr. Heelis's tone changed.

"An artist and a writer," he said. "Of course my poor opinion can't mean much, but to me, I'd say you're quite remarkable, miss."

Beatrix felt a wash of warmth flow through her body. Mr. Heelis, leaning against a tree, was smiling at her. She looked away. Try as she wished, she couldn't dare look back.

A short while later, they were all back on the cart road returning to the estate. Beatrix walked beside Mr. Heelis, her heart pounding, her eyes blurring, at being so near to him. She wanted the walk to be over so that she could breathe again, and yet, as the estate came into view, she felt a panic that the walk would actually come to an end.

Thankfully, Mr. Heelis asked her about herself, which allowed her to talk without revealing her dangerous feelings.

"I always loved drawing animals," she said. "But for fun I'd draw clothes on them. After that, well, the stories just happened. I don't know when it all started . . ."

It seemed to Beatrix that her heart could not be more thunderous, or her emotions more confusing or unbearable – but there was worse to come. They suddenly became aware of music, fiddles and pipers, playing nearby. In a valley below the hills was a small village, and by the slanting rays of the afternoon sun, Beatrix and Mr. Heelis could see that a country fair was in progress. The music came from an open square where dancing was in full swing.

"Well now," said Mr. Heelis, "that's the perfect end for a walk in the country. Do you know country dancing?"

"Well, I . . ." said Beatrix.

"Of course you do," said Mr. Heelis. "Every schoolgirl does. Would you believe, at sixteen I used to win prizes. Come on. We have just time for one dance."

He reached out his hand. Beatrix froze.

"What's the matter?" said Mr. Heelis.

The matter was that Beatrix's panic had leapt to a new height. This time it threatened breathing entirely.

"I don't dance. I don't know how," said Beatrix, backing away from him. She could not bear being so close to him.

"Well then, aren't you in luck!" said Mr. Heelis. "It happens that I'm an excellent teacher."

Beatrix pulled further away. "No, no . . . I . . . Another time I will." She retreated back to the road.

They walked on toward the estate.

"I'm sorry, miss," said Mr. Heelis, after a moment. "The dance. That suggestion was out of place."

"Oh no," said Beatrix. "It was a very lovely thought. Please don't feel . . . ever . . ." She didn't know how to finish her sentence.

They had come to a path that veered off from the road. "Beg pardon, miss," said Mr. Heelis, "I really must take this path this very minute. See – there's Sarah waiting." Down the path by a small cottage was a young woman, standing by a gate. "She's going to be furious I'm so late," he said, and then added with pride, "Sarah's my fiancée."

"Your fiancée?" said Beatrix.

"Yes," said Mr. Heelis. "We're to be married in November. If she'll forgive me for today. Good luck with you, Miss Beatrix. With your art, and your writing, all your creative pursuits!" William Heelis waved and he and Pip bounded down the path to meet his intended.

Beatrix waved after him, and then her smile faltered. No one, not Fiona, not even Mr. Heelis, would have known, looking at her, that inside her was such deafening turbulence.

Married! Why had it never even crossed her mind?

"Very stupid duck," she said to herself.

In the warm afternoon sunlight in Kensington Gardens, Beatrix finished her story. Much of what she actually remembered she left out of her version to Norman. "So that's how I came to invent a story about a duck," she said. "I don't know why I recalled it just now."

"It's a delightful story, that's why. Who would ever want to forget it?" Norman said. He hesitated. "And the gamekeeper?"

"I never saw him after that summer."

Norman managed to sound sympathetic. "Pity," he said.

Miss Wiggin, at the adjoining table, pursed her lips and elaborately took out a small watch from her handbag. It was time to go.

"So, Miss Potter," said Norman. "I say we must start planning new stories straightaway. Jemima Puddle-duck! The public should like that. And the other one you told me, about Tom Thumb and Hunca Munca and the dolls' house! And of course *The Tailor of Gloucester*. What do you think?"

Beatrix picked up his excitement. "If *you* think . . ."

Norman turned to her. "Your book has been very important in my life," he said fervently. "*You* have been . . . very important . . . in my life."

"And you in mine, Mr. Warne."

"And so we shall have to do it again. And again."

He took her arm to lead her out of the park. "I promise you: I intend to be a nuisance. You won't get me out of your hair! Not too easily."

Chapter Eight

In the months that followed, pages of drawings flew off Beatrix's desk in the third floor studio at 2 Bolton Gardens. It had not taken long for Beatrix to realize that as soon as she had several drawings completed, that was reason for a trip to F. Warne and Co. to show them to Norman, or to invite him to her house for a presentation over tea. And so through the spring, the pages appeared, the manuscripts thickened, and the excursions increased. The Potter family took their usual summer holiday in the country, the Lake District having supplanted Scotland as the destination of choice, and when Beatrix returned in the autumn, she had several manuscripts to deliver to her publisher. These required countless more trips to the printer, to the bookbinder, to Warne and Co., and to teas and dinners at which business could be discussed with Mr. Warne. Phrases like "I'm going out" and "I shan't be home for luncheon" became routine in the Potter house, to the increasing displeasure of Beatrix's mother.

As time passed, the window at Wilkins Booksellers had more new small volumes to place beside *The Tale of Peter Rabbit*. There was *The Tale of Jemima Puddle-Duck*, *The Tale of Two Bad Mice*, about Tom Thumb and Hunca Munca, and *The Tale of Squirrel Nutkin*, about an independent squirrel. Looking into the shop from the outside, as had become their habit, Beatrix and Norman, in one brief hour, saw more than a dozen customers pick up one book from each stack, and take them all to the counter.

"Miss Potter," said Norman, "it is time for you to accept something: Beatrix Potter has become a success."

"Oh my," said Beatrix.

Beatrix's excursions out of her house were not limited to meeting Norman Warne. A good many of her journeys were to meet his sister, Amelia. Millie invited Beatrix to tea, invited her to take walks in the Botanical Gardens, invited her to join her at lectures at the library and exhibits at the British Museum. For her part, Beatrix invited Millie to go with her to art shows and science presentations, or to attend the opera whenever the bill included something heavy that Mr. and Mrs. Potter chose to miss. Norman could not endure German operas, but luckily Millie had a tolerance for Wagner, and so Beatrix invited her. The two spinsters found that they had in common an unexpected and delightful ability to find weighty, meaningful art hysterically funny.

One day as they strolled through the brocaded walls of the National Gallery, passing painting after painting hung edge to edge, they came upon a new acquisition that had been set out on a large easel. It was a huge Rubens painting of a voluptuous nude on a velvet couch. There seemed to be acres of pink and white flesh, particularly centered on a rump of monumental proportion. Above, two merry cherubs innocently pulled back a sheet so that the body could be displayed. The mammoth young lady naked on the couch looked over her shoulder at the viewer with a blank expression that seemed to say, "Oh, is it *you?*"

Millie and Beatrix stood in front of the painting for a long serious moment.

"Lovely sense of color," said Millie.

"It's the composition, actually," said Beatrix. "Note the implied diagonals of the draperies that lead the eye to the center, to the woman's hand. Very representative of baroque paintings."

Millie's hand traced the implied line. "Yes, I see that. Very skillful."

They studied the painting for a long moment – and then burst into sputtering laughter.

"I know it's great art," Millie gasped, "but she looks so uncomfortable."

"And chilly!" Beatrix added.

It was somewhere during these visits that the two women began to talk about subjects Beatrix had never before discussed with anyone. It happened naturally and without fanfare, revelations suddenly popping into casual small talk. To any other women of her age, such talk would have been commonplace, but to Beatrix, with her limited social experience, it was startling, off-putting at first, but finally, she came to admit, refreshing and exhilarating. One day it occurred to her there was a name for this new relationship, this unexpected intimacy. She had a friend.

"When did you decide you wouldn't marry?" asked Millie. The ladies were resting on a bench in a room full of Turners during a trip to yet another gallery.

Beatrix hesitated. "Did I decide? I think it was always assumed."

Millie looked up at a painting, her eyes focused on an invisible event. "I was seventeen," she said. "I came home from a ball that Mother had forced me to attend – with Norman, my sixteen-year-old brother, dear Lord, as my escort! It wasn't that I'd had a bad time. Every swain had done his duty dance. I had had fun. I gave Norman a kiss and went into my room, and it was as clear to me as anything: I was not going to marry. Ever."

Millie paused for a moment, and then added casually, "Men scare me."

In Beatrix's mind, a scene suddenly appeared (with typical photographic clarity) of a moment she had all but forgotten. "Actually there *was* one particular moment," she said with surprise. The scene replayed itself in her head. "Mother and I were planning my twentieth birthday – well, Mother was – and after listing a few aunts and cousins, she asked me who else I wanted to invite. She started to name the usual suitors, and then she stopped. "Lionel Stokely is marrying Gwendolyn Allcott," she said, "and they are going to live at Stokely Court, which Lionel has just inherited from the Earl." And then her shoulders sank, and I knew right then, it was over. She would bring me no more suitors. And I would never marry. It shocked me, the moment was so final." She turned to her friend. "But, Millie, I felt relieved! I didn't have to worry about *that* any more. I felt . . . happy! I went into the garden and filled an entire notebook with sketches."

Beatrix had not told this story to anyone before, and its power astonished her. She held the memory in her mind for a moment. "And I've never looked back," she said. Then she turned to Millie. "What do you mean, men scare you?"

"Well," Millie said, looking for the right words. "You know."

"I don't think I do," said Beatrix.

"Beatrix," said Millie in a full voice, "don't you know what happens during sex?"

"Millie!" Beatrix exclaimed, glancing around the gallery, which was quite crowded.

Millie lowered her voice. "I don't mean that *you* have," she said. "I mean, someone must have described it to you."

"I've spent summers on a farm, Millie."

"Well . . . then you *know*!" said Millie. She thought her next sentence was self-evident, but looking at Beatrix, she realized it was not. "Would you want to do . . . that?"

Beatrix didn't reply. The two women sat silently for a moment. "I've seen a birth," Millie said suddenly.

Beatrix looked around the room. "You say the most outrageous things, Millie," she said, "and always right out in public." Then she leaned close and whispered, "When did you see a birth?"

Millie leaned in too. "Our downstairs maid," she whispered loudly. "The baby came suddenly, a month early. Everyone was rushing around, so I offered to help. I went down and boiled water and tore up sheets and watched."

She paused.

"And . . . ?" Beatrix said.

"It was *horrible!* All I could think was, thank heavens that isn't me. All the delights of raising children – having them running around the house, clinging to your legs and calling you "Mama" – can't be worth that."

Millie suddenly felt she had gone too far. "I'm not a frightened person," she said. "Generally, I'm quite fearless." And then she added, "I've skied."

"You haven't," said Beatrix.

"Oh, you'd love it, Bee," cried Millie. "We could learn together. We could go to Switzerland, now that you're so rich."

Beatrix laughed. "I can see the headline in the Times: SPINSTERS KILL THEMSELVES IN FALL OFF MATTERHORN! That would be entertaining."

Millie laughed too, and then she stopped. "Unmarried women have a better life," she said. "I swear it's true. But let's not tell anyone or the secret will get out. No houses. No babies. No husbands demanding things all the time. As long as you're lucky and have one good friend . . . "

She turned towards the paintings, then turned fervently to Beatrix.

"I'm so glad Norman found you, Beatrix. I was missing something and I didn't even know."

~

The addition of friends changed more in Beatrix's life than she expected. Mornings she woke up thinking about what she was going to do that day, where she was going to go. Over the years since achieving maturity, she had progressively limited her boundaries. She gave up anticipating. She found reasons to turn down invitations, unless they were from family or family acquaintances, and soon invitations stopped coming. Beatrix retreated inside her head, where any human need for companionship was filled by her drawings. This was what produced her often misunderstood tendency to talk to her creations. She wasn't dotty, as some who observed her thought, although were she ten years older, it would have been hard to argue that talking to a painting was normal. She simply had a basic human need for personal contact, and since her animal characters assumed real and diverse personalities as they were being invented, they were there to converse with. She chastised them, corrected them, encouraged them, and – this was the part that was hard to explain – sometimes listened to them, when they gave her advice.

But now, having new human friends, she stopped talking as she drew, which, when she realized it, seemed remarkable to her. It occurred to her, moreover, that the drawings might miss her companionship. In fact, she began to feel that they might feel neglected.

Christmas was coming, and for the first time in her adult life, Beatrix thought about presents for friends. A book would do nicely for Millie, but she wanted something special for Mr. Warne. It couldn't be a purchased gift, which seemed somehow too intimate. It needed to be something both more and less personal. She decided to write him a Christmas story, one that she would give to him at Christmas, and that, if he liked, he could subsequently publish. She had made a set of paintings called *The Rabbits' Christmas Party* when she was a young woman. She could add a story and finish the set. Yes! And, she decided, she would paint a special picture of the story's central scene which she would present to Mr. Warne . . . when? The idea occurred to her that for the first time ever, Beatrix would add names of her own to the list of guests invited to the Potters' annual Christmas party.

Beatrix was in her room sketching an idea for Norman's Christmas present, a party scene with Peter and other rabbits dancing around a room in Victorian clothes. At first the characters were merely lines, then in one or two strokes, they acquired details, then suddenly personalities. Then attitudes. Then opinions.

"Why are you staring?" Beatrix said, as if correcting a child. "You're intended for someone else, not me, that's all. You are a present."

The animals seemed not at all pleased.

"Oh, now, don't give me those looks," said Beatrix. "I'm entitled to friends other than you." And then she added, "You're still my favorites."

Beatrix had intended to have Peter Rabbit smiling, but the line she drew for his mouth kept looking more like a frown. The other animals seemed to be dancing beyond her control.

"Stand still, you little imps," she said to the drawing. "Peter, you naughty boy. Look what an example you're setting! I have half a mind to paint something else."

The door opened. Mrs. Potter entered, appalled once again to find her daughter in an empty room talking to herself. On the page, the animals froze.

"There. That's better," said Beatrix, unaware of her mother's presence. "Any more of that and I'll paint you out."

"Ahem," said Mrs. Potter.

Startled, Beatrix turned to face her mother.

"What is this about extra guests at Christmas?" said Mrs. Potter.

~

In the Eagleton room at the Reform Club, his home away from the law office, Rupert Potter was thinking about art. On the table in front of him were a stack of new photographs still smelling of developing fluid. Beside them was a small volume with a cloth cover on which was printed *The Tale of Jemima Puddle-Duck*, and in a small box below, *by Beatrix Potter*. That afternoon, Rupert had strolled out to a bookshop and bought the volume. When he opened it back at the club, what he saw on the first page stunned him: a picture of a duck wearing a poke bonnet and a shawl. He sat back in his chair.

When Rupert Potter had first come to London at twenty-two to study law at Lincoln's Inn, he was a well-to-do country boy from a mill town outside Manchester. Alone in the bustling city and overwhelmed by his studies, he spent his few spare hours making sketches. He filled notebooks with landscapes, animal drawings and most especially his own personal style of caricatures. One drawing depicted a flock of ducks flying over a marsh. On a few of the ducks he had whimsically drawn hats, and on one duck in particular he had drawn a poke bonnet. Beatrix had seen these drawings, of course. From the time she was six or seven she used to spend hours looking through her father's sketchbooks, which secretly pleased Rupert more than he admitted. And now here before him was a picture drawn by Beatrix of a duck in a poke bonnet. Hers, however, was no caricature. It was refined and elegant, full of deftly expressed personality, and printed in soft colors. Seeing it in print stopped him short, and now alone in the room, he thought about art.

Rupert had always liked to draw but had no interest

in paint. Oils seemed thick and messy and imprecise. Watercolors were difficult and elusive. One had to move so quickly before the water dried and each stroke had to be exactly right the first time. A pencil sketch one could erase and correct. Perhaps that was why the new invention of photography appealed to him so. Being in black and white, it was always about line and form. The act of framing a picture in a camera lens, snapping a shutter, and then watching the picture magically appear on a blank sheet of photographic paper submerged in a pan of developing solution, never lost its mystical appeal for him. He loved form, and he marveled at creativity. Indeed, one of the things that he found so appealing about nineteen-year-old Helen Leech when he first met her in Manchester was her skill at producing soft and expressive watercolor landscapes. He couldn't do that, and he watched in wonder as she dipped her brush into water and then created evocative nature scenes with just a few flicking brushstrokes. It was an immense disappointment to him, although he never expressed it, that the minute Helen Leech became Helen Potter, moved into a large house in London, and became a mother and wife, she stopped painting altogether, in an instant, and devoted herself entirely to being an accepted lady of fashion.

If there was not to be art in his marriage, that did not stop Rupert from being attracted to art elsewhere. Over the years he had become friendly with John Everett Millais, the famous painter who had become notorious as a result of a scandal in which he had run off with, and married, the wife of John Ruskin. Rupert used to visit Millais's atelier and watch Millais paint, standing in awe at the artist's ease and facility. Millais, flatteringly, was impressed by Rupert's interest in photography, and from time to time he actually engaged Rupert's help. This new craft, he said, could be a godsend to a successful artist like himself who had more commissions than he had time to handle. Instead of repeated trips to a country mansion to get the details of a background correct, he could ask his friend Rupert to journey with him and take photographs, to which Millais could refer when back in his studio. On several occasions, Millais asked Rupert to photograph portrait subjects, to reduce the hours of posing. This was particularly useful with portraits of very busy men, and once in 1884, Rupert photographed Prime Minister William Gladstone for a Millais portrait that was going to be hung in the House of Commons. Rupert recalled marveling as he watched Millais turn the unforgiving accuracy of his photograph into a softer, richer, more humanized oil painting.

And now Rupert sat looking at a picture of a duck.

Rupert was thinking about art because he had just received a note from his wife requesting that he come home directly at the end of his workday. Rupert had received several of these notes over the years, and he had come to know what they meant. Some unpleasant or unpopular decision needed to be made, and his wife, who, as a matter of course, generally made all decisions peremptorily and without discussion, wanted him to come home and be "the man of the house." Rupert didn't like being decisive, or making difficult decisions. He was willing to be "the man of the house" when he had to be, and he felt he did it rather well, but it always left him feeling uncomfortable and unfulfilled, as if he had been giving an unsatisfactory acting performance. Instead of art, Rupert had chosen responsibility. He had a responsible profession, the law, which, in truth, he wished would simply go away. And now, responsibly, he would go home and be responsible. Rupert knew the truth. A man of his wealth and class could not pursue a career in art. And in honesty, how good would he actually have been?

~

Sure enough the air was full of tension when Rupert arrived home at Bolton Gardens. Taking off his overcoat and knocking snow off his boots and hat, Rupert could see that his wife was awaiting him in the drawing room. Beatrix was coming down the stairs.

"Hello, Father," said Beatrix. "Did you have a good afternoon at the club?"

"Don't I always?" he replied.

He led his daughter in to join his wife. "Now what is this trouble?"

Mrs. Potter spoke with an even tone. "We seem to have a situation, Rupert. We need your resolution."

Here it comes, thought Rupert.

Beatrix said, "I want to invite Norman Warne and his sister to our Christmas party."

Mrs. Potter interrupted. "With Lady Armitage, Rupert? With Sir Nigel and Sybil? A tradesman, Rupert. How will anyone have fun?"

"Norman Warne is the man who publishes my books," said Beatrix. "Mother said it's going to have to be decided by you. What's your decision, Father?"

Rupert stood in the center of the room. Lucky for him, he thought, that he had prepared himself.

Mrs. Potter saw Rupert pause, and sensed incipient waffling. "Rupert . . ." she warned.

Rupert took a bold and unexpected tack. He changed the subject. "Come see what I bought, princess."

Mrs. Potter began to fear a digression. "Rupert, stay to the point," she said.

Rupert took a package from his overcoat pocket. "I went into a bookshop and purchased this with good money."

He held up the copy of *The Tale of Jemima Puddle-Duck*.

Beatrix felt somehow hurt. "I don't understand," she said. "I could have given you one."

"Hugh Whitteford bearded me in the club room," said Rupert, "and rattled on for hours, you know him, jowls all aflutter." He imitated Whitteford's nearly incomprehensible Colonel Blimp voice. "Wife bought three of your girl's books for our granddaughter's nursery. Sent two to my adjutant when his baby was born. Sending some more by ship to friends in Bombay." Pretty soon the whole room was telling me of some purchase they'd made of my daughter's creation. So I thought it was time I bought one. I went right out to Hatchards. Put my money on the counter."

"But I've shown you all my books," said Beatrix.

"Yes," said Rupert, "but I wanted to *buy* one. Like everyone else. I owe you an apology, Beatrix." He walked over to her and put his arm around her shoulder.

"You *have* showed me your books, but all I saw was my little girl, still bringing me clever drawings to comment on. You're not a little girl any more. You're an artist. The real article. I would have been proud to say that about myself. Now I'm proud of you, my princess."

Beatrix felt a rush of emotion of a sort she hadn't felt since she was child. "Oh, Father!" she cried. She threw her arms round him, tears in her eyes.

Rupert felt moved too. Love, he thought. I've almost forgotten this feeling.

He looked over Beatrix's shoulder at his wife. "So I don't see any reason why we can't make a little social effort and welcome the man responsible for this blessing into our home. I think it will be good for all of us."

Mrs. Potter pursed her lips and her body went rigid. "Merry Christmas, Rupert," she said, and turned and left the room.

Chapter Nine

The Potters were Unitarian, and Unitarians, not believing in the Trinity, frowned on making an excessive fuss over the birth of Jesus. Throughout Beatrix's childhood, therefore, Christmases in the Potter home were not merry. The family did not decorate their home, as many families did, and while they sent restrained Unitarian Christmas cards and sang the new Unitarian Christmas carols, like "It Came Upon a Midnight Clear," the holiday was not the cornerstone of their year the way it was for most families in mid-Victorian England. It was Rupert, educated and indoctrinated at one of England's few Unitarian universities, Manchester New College, who mandated the Yuletide austerity in his home. Over the years, though, as bleak Christmas followed bleak Christmas while neighboring homes rollicked with holiday lights and gaiety, Rupert began to fear that his religious convictions were somehow responsible for the general and unexpected paucity of joy in his household. Other factors contributed as well to the Potters' annual holiday cheerlessness. Beatrix, who seemed particularly susceptible to London's fog and cold, almost always had a winter illness which kept her upstairs in bed on Christmas Eve. And in the Potter family, sad events like Grandmother Leech dying slowly and painfully always seemed to come along at Christmastime to cast a pall over the house.

Rupert was not therefore unhappy when, as Beatrix entered her teens and it became time to consider how to present her to society, Helen Potter decided that some holiday grandeur had to enter their life. So she began an annual Christmas party to which she invited prized guests, preferably ones with titles and eligible sons. Later, after Beatrix was no longer pursuing suitors, Helen continued the tradition because she felt, with increasing purposefulness, that it was this party that kept her connected to the center of London society.

So it was that in December of 1904, the home of the Unitarian Potters was a Victorian Christmas fantasy: a giant tree trimmed with candles and fragile glass ornaments from Germany, wreathes in the windows, a Yule log in the fireplace, pine boughs, ceramic angels and Christmas cards on the mantel, a salver with silver punch bowl and cups, servants with trays of mince pies and plum pudding and hot mulled wine. Mrs. Potter was wearing a specially designed dress of peach-colored taffeta along with her most impressive pearls and brooches as she gave final instructions to the servants.

"Don't serve Sir Nigel the punch with the brandy unless he demands it," she said to Hilda, the maid. "After dinner, he'll ask for port. Give me a little signal when he's had four glasses."

Rupert appeared looking dashing in evening clothes. "The house shimmers, darling," he said, planting a kiss on his wife's cheek. "You've done it again."

In the hall, the grandfather clock struck seven. Instantly, as if it were an extra stroke of the clock, the doorbell chimed. Hilda, the maid, opened the door to Norman and

Millie in evening clothes. There was snow on their hats and hair.

Beatrix rushed out of the dining room to greet them. "Mr. Warne! Millie! I'm so delighted. Here, let Hilda take your coats."

Their coats were whisked away. Cox, the butler, took his position at the drawing-room arch. "Miss Amelia Warne! Mr. Norman Warne!" he announced.

Mrs. Potter looked chagrined. Socially adept people did not arrive on time.

"Mother, Father," said Beatrix, "I'd like you to meet Miss Amelia and Mr. Norman Warne."

"How charming of you to be punctual," said Mrs. Potter.

The tone of the evening had been set.

Helen Potter had acted boldly to deal with Beatrix's unwanted additions to her guest list. She had filled out her own list with couples who knew each other well and who would not need to resort to the Warnes for conversation. An elegant and aristocratic group they were too, the women in dazzling embroidered gowns and hair set with jewels, the men in stiff dress shirts and evening clothes. Sir Nigel and Lady Sybil Westlake laughed at one end of the room with Robert and Diana, Lord and Lady Armitage. Mr. and Mrs. Richard Catchpole, from the Royal Academy of Science, chatted with Mr. and Mrs. Henry Williamson, Mr. Williamson being the Manchester representative in the House of Commons. Norman, Millie, Beatrix and Miss Wiggin stood together in an uncomfortable knot by the conservatory door. The Warnes, of course, knew no one at the party and, exactly as Mrs. Potter had predicted, didn't fit in. To top it all, there was the glum presence of Miss Wiggin, who affixed herself to their group as if determined to kill any chance of gaiety.

What Helen Potter didn't know is that Beatrix's excitement at having her new friends with her was so great that nothing could dampen her joy. Mrs. Potter also didn't know that dealing with stuffy and pretentious people was exactly what Beatrix and the Warnes found entertaining.

"I think we should make conversation, don't you?" said Norman, dryly. "Just like everyone else."

"Absolutely," said Millie. "These Christmas biscuits are delicious, wouldn't you say?"

"They are, aren't they," said Beatrix. "Marzipan, perhaps?"

"Mmm, yes," said Millie, popping one in her mouth.

"I'll fetch the tray," said Miss Wiggin.

"No, please, no need," said Millie. "We don't want the biscuits. We just want to talk about the biscuits."

Miss Wiggin, baffled, returned to her position.

There was a silence. A maid passed with a tray of champagne glasses. Norman noticed Miss Wiggin looking longingly at them.

"Go on," said Norman to Miss Wiggin, under his breath, "it'll do you good."

Miss Wiggin hesitated. "I suppose one couldn't hurt," she said finally, and moved a few steps away to take a glass.

"I think Wiggin is under orders never to leave our side," Beatrix whispered. "Isn't that festive?"

At long last, dinner was announced. Mrs. Potter had seated the Warnes and Beatrix apart at various points around the table, thus guaranteeing that they could do nothing but exchange looks and feign interest in the other guests' conversation, in which they were not generally included, and often outright ignored.

The dinner itself was a sumptuous, shimmering silver-and-red candlelit extravaganza. The dining table had been extended to its fullest length, and it was set with the Potters' most dazzling crystal, silverware and gold-inlaid plates. A velvet runner down the center was strewn with holly, above which a row of crystal candelabra blazed. Dinner was not only grand, it was also long. A soup course was followed by a salmon course, a pâté course, and a lobster course, following which Cox the butler rolled out a trolley and carved a huge turkey. On the trolley was also an assortment of game birds, pheasants and quail, as well as a mountain of chestnut stuffing dumplings. After this there was roast lamb. Then began several courses of desserts, ending with a Christmas pudding flambé that was paraded around the room before being served.

Helen Potter wanted the Warnes to find the evening boring, which it certainly was, but she didn't reckon on them enjoying the boredom so much. Still, it did seem to Beatrix, Norman and Millie that the dinner would never end. It took a long time before, eventually, the meal was finished and the three of them found themselves alone together at the dining-room table.

"Such scintillating conversation!" said Millie.

"Oh yes, mine too," said Beatrix. "The weather in Amsterdam in July!"

"Mr. Williamson said he didn't know *Gotterdammerung*,"

said Norman, "so Lady Armitage decided to tell him the entire plot."

"Which she got completely wrong!" laughed Millie. "Didn't she, Norman?"

"How would I know?" said Norman.

Miss Wiggin entered the room and sat quietly by the door, instantly casting her usual pall.

Norman leapt to the rescue. "Perhaps I can interest you ladies in an after-dinner coffee?"

Mrs. Potter came into the dining room, not surprised to find Beatrix and her two guests hidden away from the other guests. She took in the scene, sighed audibly and approached Norman.

"Some of the gentlemen are going to play a few hands of cards," said Mrs. Potter, with a palpable reluctance, "and they're short of a fourth. I don't suppose you play whist, Mr. Warne?"

Norman shook his head politely. "I've never had much aptitude for cards, I'm afraid."

Mrs. Potter smiled. This was exactly the answer she expected from a lout. "A pity," she said. "They'll be so disappointed."

"I play," said Millie.

There was an awkward silence.

Mrs. Potter spoke as if chastising a child. "This is to play with Sir Nigel, Miss Warne. Sir Nigel takes his whist very seriously."

Millie smiled pleasantly at Mrs. Potter, and said, "Actually, I play rather well."

"Millie . . ." said Norman, astonished at her brazenness.

Millie rose from the table. "You two have plenty to

talk about without me. And if they can't play without a fourth . . ."

Mrs. Potter was not at all happy. But she had three guests who wanted to play cards whom she did not wish to disappoint and here was a solution. "Come along, Miss Warne," she said, leading Millie away. Millie looked back over her shoulder at Beatrix and Norman as she left the room. The spinster was going on an adventure!

The sound of a piano came from an adjoining room. Lady Sybil emerged from the room and announced, "Carols in the music room, my dears."

The remaining guests flocked towards the door. Beatrix and Norman were suddenly alone in the dining room. Alone, if one didn't count Miss Wiggin. From the music room they heard:

> "God rest ye merry, gentlemen
> Let nothing you dismay . . ."

Beatrix's heart began to pound. This was the moment she had rehearsed in her mind all day, and she tried to make it sound off-hand and extemporaneous. "Perhaps, Mr. Warne," she said, "now is a good time to show you your Christmas present."

Miss Wiggin sat up in her chair, instantly alert.

"It's upstairs," Beatrix continued.

"Present?" said Norman. "I had no idea . . ." He stood up from the table, and Miss Wiggin rose too. "I'll bring the coffee," he said.

"I'll get your coffee," said Miss Wiggin.

Norman addressed her grandly. "Miss Wiggin," he said.

"I am filled with the holiday spirit. Please allow me to fetch the coffee, and – may I get a coffee for you too?"

Miss Wiggin started to protest, but Norman was too gallant to be refused. "I absolutely insist," he said. "I'll meet both you ladies upstairs."

Beatrix and Miss Wiggin headed for the stairs in the hall. Norman stopped at the side table, where a maid poured him three cups of coffee and placed them on a tray. Norman was about to follow the ladies when he saw a decanter nearby. On a whim, he added a large splash of brandy to one of the cups.

Norman sang along with the carolers, impishly.

"Oh tidings of comfort and joy, comfort and joy,
Oh tidings of comfort and joy."

With a merry bounce in his step, Norman followed Beatrix and Miss Wiggin, up the stairs.

On the landing, Norman distributed the coffee. "For you, my dear Miss Wiggin," said Norman, giving her the laced cup. "And you, Miss Potter." He whispered conspiratorially to Miss Wiggin. "I added a little brandy to ours. It's Christmas."

Miss Wiggin, who liked very few of the friends who passed through the Potter house, and in particular liked none of the people whom Beatrix encountered, had somehow changed her mind about Norman. He was always pleasant to her, always addressed her with respect, and never acted superior. Many people forgot that Miss Wiggin was from a good family. Norman seemed to treat her as if they were from the same class, she began to think, and that made her feel a kind of kinship with him that she felt with no one else. With him and him alone, she could lower her guard, relax her stiff exterior, perhaps even, on occasion, smile, as she did now when accepting a cup of coffee. She liked Norman Warne. He was a man she could trust.

This was of course a mistake.

Miss Wiggin took the cup, with an air of naughtiness. "Well, if you promise not to tell . . ." She took a sip, and the warm brandy coursed through her. "Oooh," she said, and downed the cup in one gulp.

Below, the carolers finished their song.

> "Oh, tidings of comfort and joy, comfort and joy
> Oh, tidings of comfort and joy!"

Norman and Beatrix passed the open door to Beatrix's room. The drawing table was visible inside.

"Is this where you paint, Miss Potter?" asked Norman.

"Yes," said Beatrix. "And this is where we will find your present."

They entered the studio. Miss Wiggin stayed outside the door like a sentry.

As Norman walked through the door, Beatrix felt a strange sensation.

"I think," said Beatrix, "other than Father and Bertram, you're the first man who has ever been in this room."

"Would you like me to leave?" asked Norman.

"Not in any way," Beatrix said. "Wiggin is here. And if this is the best I can do for scandal at my age, I'm hardly worthy of my reputation for creativity. Look."

On the table was a framed watercolor depicting a group of rabbits roasting apples on a fire. One of the rabbits was wearing a scarf similar to one Norman often wore.

Norman laughed in delight. "What is it?" he said.

"I'm not going to tell you," said Beatrix. "Not yet."

"Ah!" said Norman. "Secrets! At last!"

They heard a noise. Miss Wiggin, tipsy and unable to stand, had sunk to a chair beside the door.

Beatrix looked at Miss Wiggin, then looked back at Norman. "Would you like to see some of my drawings?" she said.

"Yes, indeed," said Norman. "These must be pictures no one else has seen."

"My private collection, yes," said Beatrix. "And you shall have a private showing."

Beatrix showed Norman the room. "Here, these are some of my mushroom drawings from Scotland. And these are some landscapes of the Lake District. That's the view I see every morning at breakfast. This is the first drawing I made of Benjamin Bouncer. I was, what, eight, I think." She came to a drawing she suddenly wished she hadn't put on her wall. She considered skipping over it, but Norman was caught by it.

"And this one is . . . ?" asked Norman.

"This is the first drawing I made of Jemima Puddle-duck," said Beatrix. It was the drawing she had produced on her excursion with William Heelis.

"I wonder if Jemima will like me, now I've put her into print," said Norman. He moved close to inspect the drawing, so close that he almost touched it with his nose. Jemima, in the drawing, seemed to respond to

Norman, fluttering her eyes flirtatiously at him, and preening herself.

"Jemima! Stop that!" said Beatrix.

Norman turned to Beatrix. "Stop what?"

Of course the drawing hadn't moved at all. "Just some silliness," said Beatrix. But it did seem to Beatrix that Jemima waggled her tail at Norman quite scandalously before becoming still again.

Norman continued around the room, and his eyes fell on a box with a small drawing inlaid into the top, a drawing that didn't seem to be by Beatrix. "And what's this?" he said.

"A music box," said Beatrix. "My father gave it to me for my sixth birthday. He did the drawing on it himself."

Norman picked up the box, fascinated. "I didn't know your father painted too."

"I think in his heart Father always wanted to be an artist," said Beatrix. "Of course, the family wouldn't hear of it, so he took up law. But the joke is, I've never once heard him discuss a case. He goes to his club every day, never to his office. I don't really know what he does."

Across the room, Miss Wiggin's coffee cup dropped to the floor with a loud clunk. Miss Wiggin had fallen asleep on the chair.

"Oh dear," said Norman.

"Wiggin is fallible!" cried Beatrix. "There is a Father Christmas!"

Norman and Beatrix exchanged a look. "I fear your reputation is now officially dented," said Norman. And then he added, "Perhaps we should go downstairs."

"Yes, of course we should," said Beatrix.

Neither of them moved.

Norman opened the lid of the music box. A tinkling melody began to play.

"Ah!" said Norman. "I know that tune. Very sweet. "Let Me Teach You How to Dance." Do you dance, Miss Potter?"

Beatrix felt a familiar flutter inside her. "No. No, I don't. Well, not well."

"Yes, of course. You told me," said Norman. "The gamekeeper." He smiled. "No matter. I make a terrible hash of dancing myself when I try. But the words to this tune are very sweet. You know them, don't you?"

"No, I don't," said Beatrix.

"They're actually very apt."

Beatrix wound the music box. "Would you sing them for me?" she said.

Norman suddenly felt embarrassed. But then the tinkling melody began, and unavoidably he started to sing.

> "Let me teach you how to dance,
> Let me lead you to the floor.
> Simply put your hand in mine
> And then think of nothing more."

Beatrix was surprised that Norman had a pleasant singing voice. Pleasant and . . . tender even. He looked straight into her eyes as he sang, and suddenly, to Beatrix, the room seemed to lose all its dimensions. Norman sang on.

> "Let the music cast its spell,
> Give the atmosphere a chance.

I know everything you need,
Simply follow when I lead,
Let me teach you how to dance."

The melody repeated and Norman sang the verse again, but this time he followed the directions of the words. He took Beatrix's hand. He moved close to her in the position of a waltz. As if she had no control of her body, Beatrix accepted him, putting her other hand lightly on his shoulder. Then slowly, very slowly and innocently, they began to move, in a tiny slow circle, in the middle of the carpet.

How could anyone describe the effect of this moment on Beatrix? An adolescence she had never had, a young womanhood she had never felt, came alive in her. Sensations she never imagined passed through her body for the first time ever, leaving her breathless, speechless. She suddenly felt she had blood, she had skin. She looked in Norman's eyes. She could not look away.

The melody came to an end. They stood still.

Then Norman broke the silence.

"Miss Potter," he said. "I know you have decided not to marry. All my life, I have been confident I would not marry either. But something has happened that has caused me to change my mind. I have begun to wonder if anything similar has caused you to change yours."

Beatrix attempted to speak. "Mr. Warne! I . . . I . . ."

Norman interrupted her. "Please let me go on," he said, "for if I don't say what I have to say now, I never will. Miss Potter, I . . . I should like you to consider . . . doing me the honor . . ."

"Are you . . . ?" asked Beatrix.

Norman felt a sudden panic. "I've been too presumptuous," he said. "You are happy with your current life. I've just ruined our friendship. I feel completely foolish."

Beatrix gasped. "I can't speak," she said.

"I don't expect an immediate answer."

"No, I mean, my throat," gasped Beatrix. "I can't speak. I shall need time."

Norman was confused. Was this her way of saying no? But all he said was, "Of course."

Beatrix felt her mind spin out of control. She wanted to stand before Norman, look into his eyes and tell him something simple and true, but her emotions tumbled around her, and joy, if that's what it was, crashed into thoughts that had no place. Her expectations! Her house! Her whole life! Everything that defined her seemed to lose coherence. She looked away from him, at her studio, her nursery.

"Look around you, Mr. Warne. I have lived in this room all of my life," she said in a rush. "It's a large room, isn't it? Yet a while ago these walls started closing in on me. I couldn't breathe then either. But I remembered a friend telling me that one day I should publish my stories. I thought, yes, I will take my stories out into the world. I will get myself air. But it wasn't air I was seeking!"

The door opened and Mrs. Potter entered the room. What she saw was Beatrix and Norman standing at an innocent distance from each other – but the room was definitely full of heat.

"Beatrix?" said Mrs. Potter.

Beatrix drew herself up. "I was showing Mr. Warne

his Christmas present," she said, picking up the painting from the table. "I'm an impeccably genteel unmarried lady, Mother. I haven't started to invite men to my room." She breezed past her mother. "Come, Mr. Warne, it's time for the rest of your present."

Norman passed Mrs. Potter and followed Beatrix into the hall. Mrs. Potter spotted Miss Wiggin, passed out on the chair.

"Wiggin!" she shouted, and kicked her in the shoe. Miss Wiggin woke up with a start, very confused.

"Oh, Wiggin!" cried Mrs. Potter and stormed down the stairs.

~

Beatrix, still trembling from the events in her studio, reached the ground floor just as Millie, Sir Nigel, Lord Armitage and Mr. Catchpole were returning from cards. People! she thought. Why do I have to see people now? She entered the drawing room, clutching Norman's painting and trying hard to be invisible, so that no one would speak to her. It did not work.

"What is the picture, Beatrix?" asked Lady Armitage, as Norman entered the room behind her. The room suddenly became silent.

"This?" Beatrix fumbled. "Oh, as most of you know, I've, uh, written and drawn little children's books which have been published. The man who has published them is here this evening, Mr. Norman Warne, with his delightful sister, Amelia." She gestured to Norman to join her. "To thank him for his generosity and assistance and great warm heart, well, I am writing him a Christmas story."

"Can we hear it?"

Worse and worse! Beatrix tried to close the subject but all eyes were upon her. "Oh, it isn't finished," she managed. Desperate, she looked at Millie for help. But Millie offered none.

"Oh, go on," said Millie. In truth, Millie wanted to hear the story too.

There was nothing for it. "Well, I suppose . . ." Beatrix faltered, ". . . before we part for the evening, I could share a . . . glimpse of . . ." she indicated the painting, ". . . the unfinished tale of *The Rabbits' Christmas Party*."

"Charming," someone uttered. The guests, intrigued, settled into chairs.

Helen Potter entered the room, and was dismayed to find her guests focused on her daughter.

"It is, as I say, a Christmas story," said Beatrix. "Now, I don't know if any of you know this, but –" she paused for effect – "legend has it that on Christmas Eve, between midnight and dawn, animals can talk in human speech, and some people, if they are wise enough and quiet enough, can hear them. I know such a legend exists because I made it up."

The guests laughed. "This is for you, Mr. Warne," she said. She looked straight into Norman's eyes and began her story.

"On this particular snowy Christmas Eve, a young rabbit with his two fearsome older brothers and his fiercely brave sister, set out on the journey they made every Christmas to celebrate with their friends. Rabbits are sociable creatures, so every Christmas, wherever they found themselves, they gathered for a jolly party . . ."

She continued her story, but it was not the story – not merely the story – that caught everyone's attention. Speaking slowly, gazing into Norman's eyes, shy, unworldly Beatrix Potter became transformed. Her face became radiant. She was – for the first time in her life – undeniably, unmistakably beautiful. Could anyone have ever thought she was plain?

Around the room, everyone, even those who didn't know her, sensed that something had happened.

Norman looked back at Beatrix, transfixed and enchanted.

Millie glowed. She took in Beatrix, then looked at Norman to see if he had noticed the change – and saw that he too seemed transformed!

". . . The rabbits traveled through the woods," Beatrix continued, "until they reached the burrow of their cousins, where they knew a warm fire would be waiting for them. They were welcomed in, they hung up their frosty clothes, and the party began . . ."

The servants stood in the archway, captivated.

Rupert too stared at his daughter, stunned at her confidence, mesmerized by her transformation. He looked across the room to his wife.

Helen Potter watched Beatrix in embarrassment and humiliation. That her disappointment of a daughter should be standing in front of her important guests telling a silly children's story! How long would this mortification last?

Beatrix's story came to an end. "The rabbits left the burrow, dressed in their warmest clothes, and traveled home. They had danced and eaten, roasted apples on the fire, and had talked to a human being. It was their merriest Christmas ever." She turned to the roomful of guests. "And that's the end. I apologize that I don't have all the details of the story yet. You will all have to wait until the book comes out next Christmas. But in any case, Mr. Warne will have to read it first, because he is my strict censor and . . . well, it is his present. Merry Christmas, Mr. Warne," said Beatrix, and presented Norman with his painting.

Norman came forward. "Thank you, Miss Potter. It's so beautiful," he said.

The room burst into applause.

"Here, here!" said Sir Nigel. "Good show!"

"There'll be no problem with presents for the nieces and nephews next Christmas, I dare say," said Lord Armitage.

Lady Sybil turned to Mrs. Potter. "It's lovely, Helen. It must be so satisfying to have such a clever daughter," she said.

"It's a children's story," said Mrs. Potter.

Millie came up, took Beatrix's hands in hers and kissed them. "Stunning," she said fiercely. "Oh Beatrix, how I envy you your imagination."

Beatrix looked around the room quickly. "Millie," she said, "can I speak to you a moment?"

Beatrix led Millie to the back of the drawing room and into the conservatory which overlooked the snow-covered garden. She closed the French doors behind her.

"What is it?" asked Millie. "Is there something wrong?"

"Oh no," said Beatrix. "It's simply that . . ." Her hands began to flutter. ". . . You are my first – confidante . . ."

"Ooh! And you have something to confide?" said Millie eagerly. "How delicious!"

Beatrix fumbled for words. "You and I, Millie, we're happy with our lot, aren't we?"

"What lot is that?" asked Millie.

"Being unmarried. We're free. Free of the burdens that drag down other women. Free to pursue our independent spirits and our creativity."

"Yes," said Millie. "It's a blessing from God. A secret blessing, but a blessing nonetheless. And 'spinster' is a noble word. Has something happened? Are you feeling lonely? Holidays are the hard times."

Beatrix spoke almost apologetically. "Your brother has asked me to marry him."

"*Norman?*" gasped Millie.

"And I feel quite irrationally that I . . . may accept."

"You and my brother!" Millie gasped again.

Beatrix looked deep into Millie's eyes. "I know it sounds insane, but somehow I want your approval."

"My approval?" said Millie. Her voice lowered and took on a startling intensity. "Beatrix, don't be a fool. Marry him! Tomorrow! Don't waste a moment! How can you hesitate?"

"You don't hate me?" said Beatrix.

"For God's sake, why would I hate you?"

"Both Norman and me," said Beatrix. "It would leave you alone."

Millie cried out with sudden unrestrained passion, "You have a chance for happiness, Beatrix, and you're worrying about me! I wouldn't worry about you. If a man came along who loved me and whom I loved, I'd trample over my mother. Do you love Norman?"

"Yes," said Beatrix.

"Then marry him! Don't you dare think about anyone else?"

Beatrix was abashed. "What about the blessings of spinsterhood?" she said.

"Hogwash!" cried Millie. "What else is a woman alone supposed to say? You have a chance to be loved! Take it! Leave me to be happy knowing the two people I love are happy. That's the most thought you should ever have for me."

Mrs. Potter appeared at the door.

"Our guests are leaving, Beatrix," she said. "Come see them out."

"Of course, Mother," Beatrix said. This one day had already produced more tumultuous emotions in her than she had ever experienced. She added one more. She squeezed Millie's hand. "I love you, Millie."

She and Millie returned to the drawing room, leaving Mrs. Potter alone.

"What is going on tonight?" said Mrs. Potter, aloud to the empty room. "Why do I feel a stranger in my own house?"

In the front hall, Sir Nigel and Lady Sybil were putting on their coats as Beatrix entered.

"You have a clever daughter, Rupert," Nigel said. "You must be very proud."

Rupert replied loud enough to make sure Beatrix would hear, "Of Beatrix? Yes, I am."

"To write and draw like that," Lady Sybil added.

"Beatrix should meet our niece Anne," said Sir Nigel. "Anne makes pots."

"Ceramics, Nigel," said Lady Sybil.

"Look like pots to me," said Sir Nigel.

Millie entered to get her coat and say her goodbyes. Sir Nigel stiffened. "And as for you, madam," he said, "I suggest you take up knitting!"

Sir Nigel and Lady Sybil swept out the door and down the steps to their carriage.

Mrs. Potter was horrified. "What was that all about?" she said. Had this woman somehow offended her most prized guest?

"Sir Nigel disapproves of the way I play whist," said Millie ambiguously. Then she smiled. "I'm afraid I won two guineas from him."

Mrs. Potter was appalled. Norman was embarrassed. Rupert was impressed. Beatrix was delighted.

"Come along, Millie," said Norman, putting on his coat. He turned to Beatrix's parents. "We've had the most enchanting evening, Mr. and Mrs. Potter. Thank you so much for including us."

"Beatrix wanted us to meet you," said Rupert, shaking Norman's hand.

"Yes," said Helen Potter, "at least we've accomplished that."

Millie put on her fur wrap. "Goodbye, Mrs. Potter. Mr. Potter. Sorry about Sir Nigel."

Beatrix called at the archway. "Mr. Warne, your painting!"

"Oh yes!" said Norman. "My Christmas present. I wasn't sure I was to take it."

Beatrix led Norman out of the hall back into the drawing room. She took the painting off the easel. For a moment they were alone.

Beatrix looked into Norman's eyes. "Yes!" she said.

Norman looked back in amazement. Beatrix quickly led him back to the front door. She waved as Norman and Millie went down the path to their carriage. Then she turned, passed her mother and father, and ran up the stairs like a schoolgirl.

When she reached her studio, Beatrix rushed to the window and flung it open. Down in the street, she could see the Warnes' carriage begin to move up the street. Norman, holding the painting, looked back from the carriage window. Beatrix waved. Norman saw her and waved back. The carriage disappeared.

Beatrix turned back to the room. All around were her creations, drawings, paintings, sculptures, stuffed animal versions of Peter Rabbit, Jemima Puddle-duck, Squirrel Nutkin, and all the others.

"Well, now. What do we think?" she said to her creations. "You love him too, don't you? Oh, I knew you would!"

She lifted the lid of the music box and it started to play again. She stood in the middle of the room. Her eyes closed. Her feet began to move. She sang softly to herself.

> "Let me teach you how to dance,
> Let me lead you to the floor.
> Simply put your hand in mine
> And then think of nothing more . . ."

The animals – the dolls, the drawings, the sketches – seemed to be watching Beatrix as she danced. Some were surprised, some concerned, some amazed. A few smiled. Jemima Puddle-duck beamed. On the music box, the mice

Tom Thumb and Hunca Munca seemed almost to be dancing with her.

> "Let the music cast its spell,
> Give the atmosphere a chance.
> I know everything you need,
> Simply follow when I lead,
> Let me teach you how to dance."

Beatrix, dancing with eyes closed, couldn't see her friends. She could only imagine.

Chapter Ten

Some days later, after the holidays had passed, a carriage drove through the snow to Pall Mall and stopped outside a distinguished looking building. The door opened and Norman Warne emerged.

He climbed the imposing stone stairs. A brass plaque beside the entrance read "The Reform Club". He entered the building through the heavy oak door. Inside, a footman greeted him.

"Sir?" said the footman.

"I have an appointment to see Mr. Rupert Potter in the Eagleton Room," said Norman.

"Mr. Potter is expecting you," said the footman. "Second floor, the second door on your right."

"Thank you," said Norman.

Norman ascended the ornate staircase and found himself in a corridor lined with portraits and suits of armor. He found the second door on the right, and stopped before it. The grandfather clock next to the door showed eleven o'clock exactly. Norman dried his sweating hands on his coat.

"Courage, Norman," he muttered to himself. "It's just her father."

He swallowed hard, and knocked.

From inside he heard Rupert Potter's voice. "Come in," said Rupert.

Norman opened the door, entered the room, and closed the door behind him.

The minute hand on the grandfather clock moved to five past eleven. The door to the Eagleton Room opened again. Norman emerged.

"Thank you so much for taking this time from your busy day, Mr. Potter," said Norman.

"Goodbye, Mr. Warne," said Rupert from inside the room.

Norman closed the door. From the look on his face, whatever had happened in the room was awful.

~

In the Potter house that afternoon, Beatrix ran down the stairs and turned towards the library. She had been summoned. Nervous beyond words, she slid open the library doors. Her parents were there, Mrs. Potter seated, Mr. Potter standing by the fireplace. Formality was in the air.

"Please be seated, Beatrix," said Rupert.

Beatrix closed the library doors behind her.

The grandfather clock in the hall showed 4.30. The clock hands moved to 4.35, then to 4.40, then to 4.45. Servants passed in the hall, doing their usual tasks.

Suddenly from inside the library, voices were heard. Loud voices, rising and becoming more and more heated. An argument.

Hilda, the maid, stopped on the stair and looked at Glenys, who was coming in from the drawing room. Jane, dusting the banister rail, stopped work and looked up.

Raised voices? This never happened in the Potter house.

A few sentences were audible.

Mrs. Potter's voice was heard saying, "It's out of the question! Let's hear no more of it."

Beatrix's voice answered, "I said I will do it and I will!"

The servants stalled their tasks so they could overhear.

Miss Wiggin came down from upstairs. She too heard the commotion. She clucked at the servants to resume their work. They did. But they didn't leave. Miss Wiggin herself lingered at the newel post.

The library doors were flung open. Beatrix rushed out, followed by her mother and father. The servants, having no convenient way to leave, simply remained, pretending to be invisible. Miss Wiggin disappeared into the parlor. Beatrix started up the stairs.

Mrs. Potter stormed after her. "Norman Warne is a tradesman, Beatrix!" she cried. "A Potter cannot marry into trade, and that's final."

Beatrix stopped halfway up the stairs. "And what are we, Mother? Father's money comes from Grandfather's printing mills in Lancashire. A trade, Mother! If Grandfather hadn't run for Parliament, we'd still be living in the Midlands in the shadow of his factories. And your legacy came from Grandfather Leech's cotton trade. When did we get so high-and-mighty? We're parvenus, Mother. Social climbers."

She continued up the stairs.

Rupert turned on the servants. "Why are you loitering? Find somewhere else to work."

The servants scattered.

Mrs. Potter called to Beatrix up the stairwell. "Your

father and I will not allow this marriage. It is for your own good. And there is no reason to become insulting."

"It's not an insult, Mother," called Beatrix from the landing above. "It's the truth. Our life is pretension and social aspiration. Sir this and Lady that. Norman Warne is a gentleman of comfortable means, and he is not one inch beneath us. And I intend to marry him."

Mr. Potter raised his voice. "Not if you expect to take one penny of your inheritance!" he cried.

"Happily," said Beatrix, "I am a published author. I have means of my own. This discussion is over!"

Beatrix started towards her room, but turned back, and called down the stairwell. "Canon Rawnsley told me that publishing my stories would give me freedom. I didn't realize the most important was freedom from your permission!" Beatrix continued up to her room and slammed the door.

Rupert and Helen Potter looked at each other.

"I'll go up and have a further word with her," said Rupert, after a moment.

Helen tossed her head in dismay. "Oh, you'll be a marshmallow as always. Go, Rupert! Make this the first time in your life you don't soften!"

~

Rupert knocked on Beatrix's door.

"Come in, Father," said Beatrix from inside.

Rupert entered.

Beatrix was standing by the window. She glanced at him. "Why is it after any difficult moment Mother always sends you?"

"She didn't send me," said Rupert. "I don't like tension in the house. I want to resolve this matter."

"You can't," said Beatrix. "My mind is made up."

Rupert approached her. "Your mother wants what is best for you, as I do, Beatrix. This ill-conceived marriage is not best for you."

"And you and mother are no longer young," said Beatrix. "Now that Bertram is away so much, we three are the family. As a practical matter, I run the household. As the years pass you will need me more and more to care for you. You can't afford to have me marry and leave, can you, Father?"

"You surely don't think we would deny you happiness because we need a nursemaid?" said Rupert. "That's a knife in my heart."

"But you have come to count upon your unmarried daughter. That's why God put spinsters on this earth. To stay home and care for the old folks." She turned to Rupert with sudden passion. "When was it decided that I was to be one of those women?"

"You can't make us the villains," said Rupert. "Your mother trotted out countless suitors, all . . . suitable. You rejected them all. It was you who announced at ten that you would never marry."

"That's what haunts me, Father!" cried Beatrix. "I can't trace how it happened. I didn't want to be a silly woman, keeping a house, planning teas and thinking about clothes all day. I didn't want to tie myself to a stupid man who was only in my life because he was rich enough to take care of me. I had my drawing pad and my imagination. But does that mean that I am not ever to be loved?" The cry came from the deepest part of her heart. "Tell me, Father!"

Rupert had no answer.

In the open doorway, Mrs. Potter appeared. For her too there was nothing to say.

Chapter Eleven

The next day dawned to an unnatural stillness in the Potter house. Mr. and Mrs. Potter shared a silent breakfast in the morning room. The place set for Beatrix was conspicuously empty.

Beatrix had sent word she wished to have breakfast in her room. Now she descended the stairs, carrying a tray with her breakfast dishes. Mr. and Mrs. Potter saw her as she passed on her way down to the kitchen. No one spoke. Frost was in the air. Hilda appeared, took the tray, and Beatrix went back up to her room.

~

Later that afternoon, Beatrix strode across the ornate marble floor of the Royal Westminster Bank, followed by a sour Miss Wiggin, who could barely keep up with her. She reached an imposing door, beside which sat a young man.

"Will you tell Mr. Cowperthwaite that Miss Beatrix Potter wishes to see him," she said.

The secretary disappeared into the inner office and returned immediately, holding the door to invite Beatrix in.

"Miss Wiggin, wait here, please" said Beatrix, peremptorily. She went inside.

In the warm oak-paneled office sat an officious middle-aged man who rose quickly to greet her.

"Miss Potter, this is a pleasant surprise," said the bank manager.

Beatrix came right to the point. "Ever since Father arranged for you to receive my royalty income, Mr. Cowperthwaite, I've never asked how much money I have. Do I have enough to . . . Do you think I might, at some stage, be able to afford . . . a house of my own in the country?"

Mr. Cowperthwaite leaned forward in his chair. "Miss Potter, you have enough to buy an estate. Several estates," he said. "And a house in town. You're quite a wealthy woman, Miss Potter."

Beatrix was shocked. "Am I truly?"

The secretary returned with a large ledger book with "Miss Beatrix Potter" embossed on it, which he placed on the manager's desk.

"Moreover," Mr. Cowperthwaite went on, "the income has become quite regular. There's little doubt your fortune will continue to grow. You should have no financial worries for the rest of your life."

"Extraordinary!" said Beatrix. And then she said it again. "Extraordinary!"

~

Another morning came and went in the Potter house. Then another. And then another. Each day, Mr. and Mrs. Potter had breakfast in the morning room. Each day the place set for Beatrix was empty. And each day Beatrix came down the stairs on her way to the kitchen, carrying a tray of breakfast dishes.

But one morning there was a change.

"Beatrix," called Rupert, as Beatrix reached the door to the kitchen stairs.

"Yes, Father?" said Beatrix.

"Please come in and sit with us."

"I'd rather not, Father."

"We have something to discuss," said Rupert. "A . . . proposition."

"And for heaven's sake, Beatrix," said Mrs. Potter, "let the servants carry down your dishes."

Hilda appeared from the kitchen and took the tray. Beatrix entered the morning room. Rupert indicated her usual chair. Beatrix reluctantly seated herself.

Hilda returned to remove the breakfast plates.

Mrs. Potter stalled until Hilda left. "Tea?" she asked her daughter.

"No, thank you, Mother," said Beatrix.

"Nonsense, you always take tea," said Mrs. Potter, and poured a cup for her.

Hilda left. Rupert cleared his throat.

"Contrary to what you think, Beatrix," said Rupert, "and what you so vehemently expressed, your mother and I want you to be happy."

"We simply doubt this marriage will do the trick," said Mrs. Potter.

Beatrix pushed back her chair and leapt up.

"Helen, please!" said Rupert, with a severity his wife had never heard from him before. Rupert continued, more quietly. "Sit down, Beatrix. Please."

Beatrix returned to her chair.

Rupert went on. "What we don't want is for you to rush into something that you may later want to reconsider."

"I will not want to reconsider," said Beatrix.

"We are not convinced," said Mrs. Potter.

"Helen!" said Rupert. He turned back to Beatrix. "We are not convinced. Yet, neither have we hearts of stone. Therefore this is what we propose: you may accept Mr. Warne's engagement ring and wear it. However, we will not announce an engagement, nor can you and Mr. Warne tell anyone an engagement is pending. It must be a complete secret — even from his family. This summer, you, your mother and I will go as always to the Lake District. If, at the end of the summer, you still wish to proceed, we will announce the engagement, and you can marry with our blessing and our love."

"Why must no one know?" said Beatrix.

Mrs. Potter answered firmly, "So that there will be no public embarrassment when you change your mind."

"If!" said Rupert. "*If* you change your . . . Beatrix, if you care for this man as much as you say you do, in a few months the ardor will still be there. If your mother . . . and I . . . are correct, and this . . . 'emotion' . . . cools with time, we will have protected you against humiliation and great unhappiness."

Beatrix set her jaw. "It will not cool, Father."

"Tell the truth, Beatrix," Mrs. Potter said. "You are not sure your infatuation will last three months, are you? In your heart of hearts? And a woman at your age . . ."

Beatrix's voice took on a new edge. "The only thing

true . . . at "my age", Mother . . . is that at "my age" every day . . . matters."

She paused for a moment. Then she rose from her chair, and addressed her parents with sudden determination.

"All right, Mother, Father," said Beatrix. "I accept your terms. Mr. Warne and I might well want to wait till after the summer anyway."

Beatrix turned back when she reached the doorway.

"But use your time well, Mother," she said. "Make plans! There will be a wedding in this house come October!"

~

Beatrix had been invited to tea at the Warne home the following day, and finding a few moments alone with Norman in the conservatory, she presented the news of her parents' proposition like an ambassador returning from the enemy with terms for a truce. For a moment Norman didn't speak.

"You're angry, I know," said Beatrix. "It's such an insult. You'd be completely justified to . . ."

But Norman was not insulted. He had had a five-minute interview with Beatrix's father, at the end of which he knew conclusively that the marriage would never be allowed. Now, hearing this news, he simply said, "In the autumn? An October wedding? Lovely!"

Beatrix was astonished. "I thought you'd want nothing more to do with me," she said.

"How could you think that, Miss Potter?" said Norman. "Nine months from now, a year from now, what's that? The time isn't for us, it's for them! How can your parents know what has happened to us? They've never felt it."

If Beatrix felt love for Norman Warne before, it was as nothing compared to what she began to feel now.

"Our parents are difficult people," said Norman, "but we love them and so we will have to be understanding, and give them the time they require to come round. It needn't be so bad."

"But – in secret!" said Beatrix. "What shall we do?"

Norman laughed. "Well now, Miss Potter, I don't know exactly, but F. Warne and Co. is about to publish a new romance novel which I was required to read. It's called, I'm embarrassed to say, *Forbidden Love*. Apparently – on the evidence of the book –" he leaned in conspiratorially – "it's the best kind. Romeo and Juliet, Heloise and Abelard, Tristan and Isolde. So for a few months, let's see if such a thing really is more exciting. Perhaps your Richard Wagner will want to write a long boring opera about us. That would make it worthwhile." And then he added, "No one need know how much fun we're having."

~

And so it was that a month or so later, strolling in snow-covered Kensington Gardens, Beatrix and Norman took advantage of a moment when Miss Wiggin became distracted by children tossing out bread for a flock of birds. Norman turned so that Miss Wiggin couldn't see and gave Beatrix a small box. The box contained a ring set with diamonds. Beatrix slipped the circlet on her finger, then immediately covered it with her glove.

Later, when the first crocus peeped through the melting

snow, Beatrix, accompanied by Miss Wiggin, entered the offices of Warne and Co., and in front of the whole staff presented Norman with a sheaf of new drawings whose title page read: "The Tale of Mrs. Tiggy-Winkle". As the roomful of people marveled and gushed at the new story, Beatrix and Norman alone and connected in the crowd, smiled at each other in a way that no one in the room noticed.

Still later, when tulips and jonquils blanketed the parks, and Kensington Gardens had exploded into forsythia, Beatrix and Norman were at the print shop once again driving the printer crazy mixing colors, when Beatrix's hand accidentally touched Norman's hand. She did not move it. They pretended to be absorbed in the color mixing. The printer held up the frontispiece they were printing, a picture of a plump hedgehog washerwoman holding a flatiron. Miss Wiggin looked up from her seat a distance away, and Beatrix and Norman casually moved their hands away from each other.

When the groomed flower beds of the Gardens were abloom with early roses and irises, Beatrix, Norman and Millie, with Miss Wiggin trailing, paid another visit to Cecil Court, where Mr. Wilkins was putting a stack of new books in his shop window, next to a sign that read: "Just Arrived." In the center of the window he placed *The Tale of Mrs. Tiggy-Winkle* by Beatrix Potter. Millie, with a glance at Beatrix and Norman, lured Miss Wiggin into the shop, leaving Beatrix and Norman a moment of intimacy across the walk.

~

Finally, as spring flowers gave way to summer phlox, hollyhocks and delphiniums, it was time for the Potter family to leave again for the Lake District. The trip to Euston Station was its usual chaotic rush. The Potters' luggage filled an entire baggage cart. But this departure was more chaotic than usual because it was taking place in a downpour. A storm was blowing rain through the open spaces above the train carriages onto the covered platforms. Saunders and the porters pushed through the crowd to the baggage van, where they deposited the soaking luggage. Hilda and Jane, carrying hand luggage, moved the Potters towards their carriage.

The Potters settled into their compartment, but Beatrix lingered on the platform. Norman had said he would be there to say goodbye, but the departure time was coming fast and he was nowhere to be seen. "Come inside, Beatrix," said Mrs. Potter. Beatrix boarded the train but instantly returned to an open window, scanning the platform.

During the few seconds when she had been in the compartment, a man had passed the carriage and was now walking away from her towards the engine. It was Norman! Beatrix grabbed her umbrella and hurried out of the compartment.

"Beatrix!" Mrs. Potter cried.

Beatrix bounded off the train and ran through the rain to catch up with Norman. She reached him near the engine. "Mr. Warne!" she cried. The man turned.

It wasn't Norman.

"Oh, I'm so terribly sorry," she mumbled. Deflated, she turned back.

Inside the train, Mrs. Potter became nervous that Beatrix would be left behind. She came out of the compartment to investigate but could not locate her daughter. "Beatrix!" she cried.

A railway guard blew a warning whistle.

Suddenly down the platform ran Norman. He was not wearing a raincoat or carrying an umbrella, and was drenched.

"Miss Potter!" he cried.

"Mr. Warne!" cried Beatrix.

Norman reached her.

"I was beginning to fear you wouldn't come!" she cried.

"How could I not come?" said Norman.

"Look at you. You're soaking," Beatrix said.

"It wasn't raining when I left our offices," said Norman. "I wanted to fetch the proofs from the printer for your trip. But then this damn storm hit. I started back to the office to get my mackintosh, but I realized I'd never make the train."

"Here, get under my umbrella. You'll catch your death."

"I couldn't miss seeing you off," said Norman. "You know nothing would stop me."

"It's going to be the longest summer I've ever spent," said Beatrix.

"It's going to be the shortest!"

The railway guard whistled a second time and moved down the platform, closing train doors.

"Well . . . I suppose . . . I must now say . . ." Having no other goodbye available, she extended her hand to him.

Norman took her hand. "This is not how I wish to say goodbye to my fiancée," he said.

"I know, but . . ." said Beatrix.

The engine suddenly emitted a blast of steam that beclouded the platform and enveloped Beatrix and Norman.

They were suddenly alone, swallowed up by this white cloud. Masked by the billowing steam, Norman impulsively took Beatrix in his arms and kissed her.

Beatrix felt a shock pass through her. She abandoned all resistance, flung her arms around Mr. Warne, and kissed him as if there were nothing else in the universe.

Seconds later, the steam dissipated, revealing the two of them standing as innocently as before.

Norman took her hand with great formality. "Goodbye, Miss Potter. I look forward to your swift return."

Beatrix, her body throbbing, said. "As do I, Mr. Warne."

The train began to move.

"Quickly!" said Norman.

Beatrix jumped on to the moving train. From the doorway, still shimmering from the unexpected kiss, she leaned out of the window and waved. It was their first kiss.

"Goodbye, Mr. Warne," Beatrix cried.

Norman walked with the train, then ran with it, drenched in rain, until he reached the very end of the platform.

"Goodbye, Mr. Warne!" cried Beatrix again, as the train carried her out of the station.

Then, throwing caution away, she cried, "Goodbye, Norman!"

Norman waved from the end of the platform.

Beatrix shouted again, "Goodbye, Norman!"

The train moved away. The last thing she saw was Norman, standing on the end of the platform, in an ordinary suit, soaked to the skin, waving.

Chapter Twelve

The sensation of Norman's kiss lingered on in Beatrix for days. It seemed it might suffuse her entire summer. Rainy days became magical, sunny days idyllic. All she could think was that each passing day brought her closer to Mr. Warne, to . . . Norman. She filled her time painting landscapes and objects, making sketches for new stories; singing songs to herself — and writing to her fiancé.

Every expression of her happiness drove her mother mad.

The event of every morning was the arrival of the daily post. Cox, the butler, brought the day's letters on a silver tray. Each morning there were multiple letters from Norman. Each morning Beatrix gave back to Cox at least three letters to be mailed, each addressed to "Mr. Norman Warne". One letter she had written the previous morning, right after opening his letters; another she had written later in the afternoon, perhaps during a boat ride on the lake; another long one she would have written in the evening before retiring.

Each day, when Mrs. Potter looked out at the estate, she would see her daughter — on a point of land overlooking the lake, at the boathouse taking a rest, in the gazebo in the middle of the formal garden — take out a folded letter from Norman and reread it. Sometimes she could hear Beatrix singing to herself. It was always the same waltz.

"I think I shall be ill," she said one day to Rupert.

Rupert was busy organizing a new set of photographs and seemed not to be listening. Mrs. Potter looked at Beatrix at the far end of the lawn. "All I ever wanted," said Mrs. Potter, "was a daughter who'd grow up, marry well, and be happy. Is that so terrible? Why did God give me Beatrix?"

Beatrix varied her days with long walks in the breathtaking Lake District countryside. One day her companion was Canon Rawnsley, the local vicar, the family friend who was the first to recommend that Beatrix publish her stories, and who had made contact with F. Warne and Co.

"It was all because of you, you know," said Beatrix, as they passed down a lovely country road.

"I'm sure I simply hastened something inevitable," said Rawnsley, and then came the inevitable question that always put Beatrix to the test, "So, Miss Potter, what is new in your life?"

Beatrix was bursting, aching, to tell him about Norman, but all she could say was, "Nothing at all. Nothing special."

They passed a gate on which was a sign: Hill Top Farm. Beside it, a burly man was pounding a "For Sale" sign into the ground with a mallet.

"Hill Top Farm?" said Beatrix. "Everyone always speaks of Hill Top Farm."

"With good reason," said the vicar.

Beatrix approached the man pounding in the sign. "Sir?" said Beatrix. "Hill Top Farm. May I ask, is it a working farm?"

"Ay. Another great one falls," said the burly man. "But this one breaks your heart."

"Really? Why?" said Beatrix. Something about the man seemed familiar to her. "Ah, miss, a body'd have to be a poet, which I certainly am not." The burly man stopped for a moment.

"Excuse me, miss," he said, "but I'd swear you were someone I once knew. Your name wouldn't be Potter, by chance?"

Beatrix instantly recognized the man. "Good heavens! Mr. Heelis! Is that you?" She offered her hand and he took it.

"Well, well, Miss Potter," he said.

"Are you back caring for an estate, Mr. Heelis? Did you give up on the law?"

William Heelis chuckled. "I know how this looks, but no, I've not abandoned the law, not exactly." He held up his hammer. "A country solicitor needs to be proficient in many skills, miss. Sometimes it's law, sometimes it's real estate, and sometimes carpentry."

"And how is your wife?" said Beatrix.

"Alas, my betrothed did not become my wife. Married a damn judge rather than a student of the law. Many years ago and all that. Are you still a student of Wonders, Miss Potter? If you've never seen Hill Top Farm, I think you'll agree it qualifies. If you have the time."

"I'm sorry, no . . ." said Beatrix, and then she thought. "Actually, yes I can. Time is exactly what I do have. If it's all right with you, Canon Rawnsley."

"It's one of my favorite walks," said the vicar. William Heelis led Beatrix and the vicar up the drive.

They reached the top of the hill on which was a large country farmhouse. As they did, it became clear that Hill Top Farm overlooked one of the most spectacular views on the face of the earth.

"Not a bad outlook, Miss Potter," said Mr. Heelis.

Beatrix was transfixed. "Oh, sublime! It is truly sublime!"

Mr. Heelis watched her as she took in the view.

~

One day in midsummer, when Beatrix leafed through the morning post Cox had brought in, she was surprised to find that there was no letter at all from Norman. She put the letters back on the tray for her mother.

The next morning, it was Mrs. Potter who leafed through the day's post. Beatrix stood nearby, waiting. Rupert was having breakfast.

"Once again, no letter from your Mr. Warne," said Mrs. Potter. "Is it time for me to start feeling hopeful?"

"He said he might take a few days holiday," said Beatrix, not showing a shred of concern. "The post is no doubt slow from wherever he's gone."

Mrs. Potter came across another letter. "Here's something that appears to be from Mr. Warne's ghastly sister."

"From Millie!" said Beatrix. "How delightful!" She flaunted the letter by waving it in the air. "I shall read it out at the boathouse."

Rupert and Mrs. Potter watched as Beatrix floated across the lawn carrying her sketch pad and her paintbox and Millie's letter. Beatrix had never seemed so young, or so at ease, or so happy.

"Madame Irina, for the wedding dress, don't you think?" said Rupert.

"Rupert, really!" said Helen Potter. "That is not amusing."

"We've lost, Helen," said Rupert. "Look at her. I've never seen anyone so happy."

Rupert and Helen Potter watched Beatrix arrive at the boathouse at the end of the garden overlooking the lake, then watched her settle in, lean against the railing, and open her letter.

They heard a loud crash. In the boathouse, Beatrix had dropped her paintbox and sketchbook.

Beatrix ran out of the boathouse, and up the lawn. She rushed across the terrace, past Mr. and Mrs. Potter.

"Norman is ill!" she cried.

She disappeared into the house, dropping Millie's letter as she went. Rupert picked up the letter and read it.

A servant ran from the house to the stable. Moments later, the carriage arrived at the front door. Beatrix flew out of the house wearing a coat and carrying a small bag, passing Mr. and Mrs. Potter at the door. She climbed into the carriage.

"Stop her, Rupert," cried Mrs. Potter. "She is not to go!"

"For God's sake, Helen," said Rupert, "it's her fiancé!" He made a quick decision. "I'll get my coat and go with her."

Before he could move, however, the carriage leapt forward and disappeared down the drive.

~

A train belching smoke slashed through the magnificent Lake District landscape, back to London. Inside a compartment, Beatrix sat in deathly stillness. Miss Wiggin was not with her. For the first time in her life, she was traveling alone.

~

Beatrix arrived at Euston Station and found a hackney cab to drive her to Bedford Square. The carriage drove up to the Warne house. The driver helped her out. Beatrix went to the door. It was strange to be at this door with no one opening it the moment she appeared, no one waiting to greet her. She lifted the door knocker and knocked. The door was opened after a few seconds by a servant with a drawn face whom Beatrix didn't know. This too was strange.

"Yes?"

"I'm . . . Beatrix Potter," Beatrix said. It was all so . . . odd.

Norman's brother Harold appeared at the door. "Ah, Miss Potter," he said in a subdued voice. "Please . . ." He gestured for her to come in.

"I came as soon as I . . ." Beatrix stammered.

"Yes," said Harold, "it's very kind of you. Very kind indeed."

"Kind"? thought Beatrix. "Kind"? The word was meaningless to her. "How is Mr. Warne?" she managed.

Millie's voice came from inside. "Beatrix! You've come!" Millie appeared at the door, gaunt, red-eyed and looking suddenly old. She pushed past Harold and embraced Beatrix, holding on to her as if for dear life.

"Oh, Beatrix! Beatrix!" Millie cried.

"What is it, Millie?" said Beatrix. The realization began to hit. "What is it, Millie? Tell me!" She looked into Millie's face. "Millie!"

~

"He was so happy, Beatrix," Millie said, as they stood in the garden. "He sang songs around the house. He made me dance with him in the parlor. He laughed, Beatrix, all the time! Everyone noticed the change. Of course, only I knew the reason. But all summer, he had a cough that wouldn't go away. Then the cough got worse, and in one night he was gone. It was horrible! I keep thinking it hasn't happened. I keep expecting to meet him in the hall."

"Oh, Millie!" cried Beatrix. She hugged Millie and then said, "When is the funeral?"

Millie answered with great difficulty. "It was yesterday."

"Yesterday!" cried Beatrix. "I can't . . . see him?" Tears welled in her eyes.

"It was just the immediate family," said Millie. "I couldn't . . . think of a way to ask them to delay for you."

Norman's brothers, Fruing and Harold, came into the garden.

"It was very kind of you to come and pay your respects, Miss Potter," said Harold. Kind! That word again! thought Beatrix.

"We know you made a lengthy trip," said Fruing Warne. "We are all very touched. Our mother is particularly moved, and is so sorry she isn't well enough to come down to greet you."

"Mr. Warne was . . ." Beatrix began, but she did not know how to finish the thought.

"I'll be taking over my late brother's business affairs, Miss Potter," said Harold. "I want to assure you that F. Warne and Co. will do everything in its power to ensure that our tragic loss will cause you the least possible inconvenience."

"Inconvenience?" said Beatrix.

"Please accept the gratitude of the entire family," said Fruing.

There was an awkward silence. No one moved.

Harold broke the silence. "Of course, stay with Amelia as long as you like, Miss Potter. I do believe she needs companionship in this dark time."

Fruing and Harold made little bows, and went back into the house.

Beatrix became wild-eyed. "They want me to leave."

"No!" said Millie. "No!"

"Yes, they do!" said Beatrix. "I'm an author they publish and it's so kind of me to pay my respects, but now it's time to leave! It's as if it never happened!" She picked up her bag.

"Beatrix!" cried Millie.

"I can't stay in this house, Millie. I'm sorry. I want to be with you now, but I have to leave. No one knows about us here. We've been erased, Norman and I. We never existed."

Beatrix ran from the garden, through the drawing room and out of the Warne house, forever.

~

Returning to 2 Bolton Gardens, Beatrix walked unsteadily up the steps. Hilda, the maid, greeted her at the front door.

"Miss Beatrix! What are you doing in London?"

Beatrix walked past Hilda without speaking and started up to her room.

"Begging pardon, miss," said Hilda, "but is something wrong?"

"A friend died, Hilda," said Beatrix, without stopping.

"Oh, I see," said Hilda. She called up to Beatrix, "It's awful to lose a friend. Was she a close friend?"

Beatrix entered her room. She dropped her coat, her bag and her hat on the floor. She stood in the middle of the room, helplessly. Where was she to go?

She looked around the room. All around were her animal creations, drawings, paintings, completed books — and dolls, stuffed animals of Peter Rabbit, Flopsy, Mopsy and Cotton-tail, Tom Thumb and Hunca Munca, Jemima Puddle-duck, Mrs. Tiggy-winkle. They seemed to look back at Beatrix, with wide-open blank glass eyes.

Beatrix clenched her fists and screamed at them. "What good are you now?" she cried.

Beatrix sat down in a big rocking chair near the window. She stared out at the sky. Then she closed her eyes.

A stuffed doll of Peter Rabbit watched her with particular concern. Peter's glass eyes glazed over. They seemed to fill with tears. Tears in a doll's eyes? Impossible! If Beatrix were looking, she would have seen it was impossible. But her eyes weren't open.

And so neither did she see it when Peter suddenly moved. Miss Potter was his creator, his friend, and now she needed comforting, he thought. He jumped off the bookshelf, approached Beatrix's chair, and with one big hop, jumped on to Beatrix's lap. He snuggled against her. Beatrix, eyes closed, knew who he was, and why he had come. She put her hand on his fur and stroked him, taking comfort from him.

Did she need her friends so much that she could give dolls life?

In her mind, the other animals in the room saw what Peter had done. They too jumped off their bookshelves, bureaus, window sills. They too made their way to the chair and jumped on to Beatrix's lap. They pressed themselves against her body, cuddled up against her, burrowed under her arm so that she was holding them. Mrs. Tiggy-winkle reached up and brushed her paw tenderly against Beatrix's cheek. Beatrix's lap and arms and shoulders became filled with creatures comforting her. Beatrix responded to them without opening her eyes, gathering the animals in her arms, hugging them all. Tears were rolling down her cheeks.

~

Later that evening, Hilda came up the hall stair, carrying a tray of food for Beatrix. She went to the door of Beatrix's room, knocked lightly, and opened the door.

Beatrix was asleep in the rocking chair. She was clutching a lapful of stuffed animals.

Chapter Thirteen

Morning sunlight poured in through the hallway windows as Hilda came upstairs to Beatrix's room carrying a breakfast tray. She knocked at the door.

"Beg pardon, Miss Potter. I have your breakfast."

Beatrix's voice came from inside. "Leave it there."

Hilda placed the tray on the floor. "And, miss, will you be needing the carriage to take you to the station?"

There was a long silence.

"I won't be going to the station."

Hilda had been in the Potters' employ for almost twenty years. It was never a requirement for her to have feelings for her employers, but in this moment Hilda realized that she cared about Miss Beatrix.

"Are you well, miss?" said Hilda.

"I'm fine," said Beatrix. "I just have a headache."

"Can I get you anything, then?"

"Nothing," said Beatrix. "And don't disturb me again, Hilda."

"Very well, Miss Potter," said Hilda. Concerned, she returned downstairs.

Inside the room, Beatrix, sat motionless in the rocking chair, in the same clothes and the same position she was in the night before, still clutching her armfuls of stuffed animals. Tear-streaks had dried on her face.

Beatrix began to rock back and forth slowly.

~

That evening Hilda and Jane climbed the stairs again, bearing a new tray of food. The maids saw that the breakfast tray hadn't been touched. Jane knocked on the door.

"Your dinner, Miss Potter," said Jane.

"For pity's sake!" Beatrix shouted. "Leave it there and go away! I told you not to disturb me!"

Hilda, drawing on her much longer tenure than Jane, felt she had earned the right to step out of line. "You're not eating enough, begging your pardon, miss. That's what's causing these headaches, if you ask me."

"Go!" screamed Beatrix.

Jane and Hilda exchanged looks.

"As you wish, miss," Hilda said, so softly it couldn't be heard.

~

To servants in the Potter house, the Potters were not the best family to work for, but they were far from the worst. If the daily schedule was dull, and Mrs. Potter excessively meticulous, at least the days were regular. But since Christmas, the household had careened. There were fights, tantrums, meals taken in one's room in anger, and the worst crime of all, the breaking of routine.

But now! Beatrix returning home alone in midsummer, locking herself in her room for days! The Potters had always been a strange family, but this was oddness indeed.

In her darkened room, Beatrix sat motionless. It was the

utter brutality of it all that had disoriented her. Norman was *there*, totally there – in her mind and plans every waking hour of every day – and then he was gone, totally and cleanly, like a page ripped in one stroke from a scrapbook. What was she to do? It was beyond comprehension, beyond the capacity of the brain of one unworldly woman whose inner being had just been reconfigured by new emotions. Beatrix's response was, therefore, perfectly understandable. In the darkened Potter house, empty save for a few servants floors below, Beatrix Potter simply went mad.

It began with a sudden impulse to pace. She rose from her chair, spilling the stuffed animals on the floor, and began to walk, back and forth, back and forth, talking to herself as if solving something. But what was she solving? She didn't know.

Downstairs, the servants preparing the house for the night heard her, and looked up at the ceiling. The footsteps in Beatrix's room thumped back and forth with a desperate nervous energy. The servants could even hear Beatrix muttering to herself. Later, Hilda woke in the middle of the night and went upstairs to check on her young mistress. The heavy pacing was still continuing.

Stage two of Beatrix's madness began when Beatrix froze for an instant during her pacing, then rushed to her easel and started to dab furiously at the sheets of paper, manic and driven. Paintbrushes clattered, paint splattered everywhere. She began to draw, to write new stories, to create new characters. She couldn't make her fingers move fast enough.

The following morning, as sunlight lit up the house,

Beatrix was still at work in her darkened room, curtains drawn, still in the same clothes, still furiously painting and ranting to herself. She was bedraggled and covered with paint; her spattered hair hung in lank strips over her face. The floor was littered with drawings and half-finished crumpled pages.

In stage three, Beatrix started talking to the creatures she was drawing.

This was not like her usual conversation with her drawings, which was always mostly mere noise for companionship. This was engagement. "No, Miss Moppet, you will not have a coat, a ribbon will do for you. I don't care that the mouse has a jacket. He's a mouse." "That's the point, Tom Kitten, you've grown too fat for your tuckers. Well, you have!" "It is just a beetle, Mrs. Tittlemouse, it will merely track a little dirt across your clean floor."

In stage four, the animals began to talk back.

"Finish my legs!" cried out Mr. Jeremy Fisher. Beatrix was drawing a well-dressed frog named Mr. Jeremy Fisher but had discarded a drawing of him before sketching in his legs, and now he could not move off the page. "Have a little kindness, Mr. Fisher," said Mrs. Tittlemouse. "Poor thing's still in mourning." "Can't be in mourning," shouted Squirrel Nutkin. "It's afternoon!" "Finish me, will you please, madam," cried Mr. Jeremy Fisher. "So sad! Life is so sad," said Jemima Puddle-duck, "but can't give into it. Cheer up, I say. Can always lay new eggs." "Be quiet, you silly goose," said Beatrix. "I'm a duck," said Jemima grandly. "I need legs!" cried Mr. Jeremy Fisher. "I'm a frog! Ever hear of frog's legs?"

Other characters began talking too – not just to Beatrix

but to each other. From the floor, Beatrix could hear called-out conversations, as characters on one page talked to characters on another. "Put a sock in it, you silly thing," said Mrs. Tiggy-winkle to Jemima Puddle-duck. "Everybody leaves," said Jemima. "Can't stop people leaving. Must find new nests!" "Home is all that matters!" cried Samuel Whiskers. "Pay attention to me!" said Ptolemy Tortoise. "An Alderman knows things." The individual voices began to be lost in a general cacophony of twittering, babbling, burbling, chattering, clattering. The noise level began to rise.

In stage five of her madness, the drawings began to move.

So many images flew through Beatrix's mind, there were so many choices of pose and position, that it seemed before she could even draw one, the image moved on to a new position, and then another, and then another. She could not keep up. The succession of images blended into each other until, like the novelty book in which a child flips through pages with one finger, they became motion. She was drawing Mr. Jeremy Fisher, but before she could capture one pose, Jeremy moved – and so she tore off that page and started again. The room became even more littered with pages, and – Beatrix was sure she saw this – the images kept moving on the pages even after she threw them on the floor, calling furiously to each other.

In stage six, her drawings started to leave their pages.

The moment Beatrix added a final line to a drawing of Peter Rabbit, as she was about to bring brush to paper to add another stroke, Peter jumped out of the way. He was trying to evade her, to separate himself from her. At first

Beatrix thought it was some sort of half-serious game, and chased him over other drawings. Peter hopped across the stranded Mr. Jeremy Fisher, who waved his arms wildly to attract Beatrix's attention. "My legs! For the love of . . . !" But Peter was not playing a game. He wanted to get away from Beatrix. "I don't want you to finish me!" he cried. "I don't want to be near you!" "Come back this instant, Peter," cried Beatrix. "I'm warning you – come back or I'll make you ugly!"

The twittering cacophony became louder and louder. Painting furiously, Beatrix glanced at the floor. It was teeming with characters moving on discarded pages, teeming with paintings that had come alive. Discarded paintings, four or five deep, formed a carpet of wriggling, chattering life. The noise became deafening.

Beatrix put her hands over her ears. She grabbed Mr. Jeremy Fisher's drawing and began to finish the legs.

From downstairs came Hilda's voice, raised as loud as Beatrix had ever heard it.

"Miss! Miss! I told you, she is not to be disturbed! She's . . . oh dear, not upstairs! Miss, she is not at home!"

"She is at home for me! I need to see her." It was a voice Beatrix knew well.

"No, miss. You can't . . . "

Footsteps reached the landing outside Beatrix's room. There was a pounding on the door.

"Beatrix! It's Millie."

All the animal characters froze on their pages. Beatrix froze too, brush in hand, and listened.

Millie stood at the closed door. Hilda came up behind her. "I know I'm unannounced, but they sent back all my messages. I'm so lost, Beatrix. You're the only one I can talk to. Please, please let me in."

There was an agonizingly long moment, and then the door unlocked and opened.

Beatrix appeared framed in the darkened room. In the hallway light, it was suddenly clear how truly haggard she looked: stringy hair, gaunt cheeks, tear-stained eyes. Millie recoiled.

"Beatrix!" Millie cried.

"Millie," said Beatrix. "You look awful."

~

Millie threw open the window curtains in Beatrix's room. The sunlight blinded Beatrix, but revealed the immense squalor in which she had been living.

"You'll stay with me at Bedford Square," said Millie. "It's living in this room that's made you ill."

"I'm not ill," said Beatrix. "I just say I am, to stop questions."

Millie looked at the litter of paintings on the floor. "Isn't this the room where the walls were closing in on you? How can you hide away in this place?"

"Where am I to go?" said Beatrix. "I live with my parents. Half the year here, half the year in the country. How can I return to them and endure their unspoken – yet deafening – relief at my tragic misfortune? At least here in the dark I have my friends."

"Friends?" said Millie. "I never understand half of what you say. Get dressed. The first thing I must do is get you bathed and dressed and out into the sun."

Above: Mrs. Potter (Barbara Flynn) takes the country air with her children Beatrix (Lucy Boynton) and Bertram (Oliver Jenkins)

Below: The adult Beatrix (Renée Zellweger) works at her painting

Beatrix (Renée Zellweger) decides to become an author

Below: Publishers Fruing and Harold Warne (David Bamber and Anton Lessing) negotiate with Miss Potter

Above: Beatrix (Renée Zellweger) and her editor
Norman Warne (Ewan McGregor) look at
The Tale of Peter Rabbit, hot off the press

Below: Over tea Beatrix and Norman
discuss the astonishing success of her book

Norman's sister, Millie (Emily Watson) visits an art gallery with Beatrix

Left: Beatrix (Renée Zellweger), Millie (Emily Watson) and Norman (Ewan McGregor) at the Potters' Christmas party. Behind them, the ever-watchful chaperone Miss Wiggin (Matyelok Gibbs) looks on

Right: The perfect hosts, Helen Potter (Barbara Flynn) and her husband Rupert (Bill Paterson), welcome their guests

Above: Norman (Ewan McGregor) makes his proposal to a surprised Beatrix (Renée Zellweger)

Below: Alone in her room after the party Beatrix is elated by the evening

Left: Masked by steam from the departing train, Beatrix (Renée Zellweger) and Norman (Ewan McGregor) say a fond goodbye

Above: Beatrix paints compulsively as she tries to come to terms with a terrible blow

Below: The tranquility and beauty of the Lakeland scenery give Beatrix comfort

Solicitor William Heelis (Lloyd Owen) shows Beatrix a property for sale

Below: William and Beatrix (Renée Zellweger) walk together in the countryside

Millie took Beatrix on a trip. It was a hot summer day, and Beatrix almost didn't notice where they were.

"I feel so lonely, Millie," said Beatrix. "All my life, I've been alone, yet I never once felt lonely. I've always had my painting and my writing. Now, I . . . they don't . . . Oh Millie, it's the pretending!"

"What do you mean?" said Millie.

"No one knows!" cried Beatrix. "I feel such pain in my heart — yet I must pretend that nothing has happened. "Is anything wrong, Miss Potter?" says the housekeeper. "Just a headache," I say. "I'll be fine," I say. But it's a lie! I want to run through the streets and cry, "I loved Norman Warne!" I want people to stop and say, "There's Miss Potter, isn't it tragic? She lost her love." Then I think, how selfish of me to feel that way. Norman died. Not me. But in a way, I died too, Millie! I died too! And I want people to know! I want their pity!"

"Here's what I say you should do," said Millie. "Stay the rest of the summer with me. We can take long walks and tend the house and pretend Norman is still there."

"But he isn't there, Millie. He's here."

The trip Millie had brought Beatrix on was to Highgate Cemetery. Beatrix's mind snapped back into focus as she beheld the freshly planted earth and wilted flowers, and the temporary headstone with Norman's name on it.

This is reality, thought Beatrix. I am facing it for the first time. She turned to Millie.

"I've spent my life pretending things, Millie," said Beatrix. "It's all I really know how to do. But Norman was real – and because we were a secret, he lives now only in my mind. I have to keep him real – in my mind. So therefore I can't pretend anything. Don't you see, Millie? If we make his death a fantasy, then loving him must have been a fantasy. And then I'll have nothing."

"So, you can't stay in my house, can you?" said Millie. "Even though I need you so much."

"It's Norman's house too," said Beatrix. Suddenly, what she had to do became vividly clear to her. She looked into Millie's eyes. "Millie, I must leave all this."

"I know," said Millie, pulling away. "And you must do without me. You must find your own way."

"Yes," said Beatrix. "My own way."

The moment hung in the air. Millie suddenly feared for her. "Where will you go?" she said.

In her head, Beatrix suddenly heard a song, a song she had forgotten, ringing out in a man's loud clear voice, echoing off the surrounding mountains. It was a song about the beauty of the England countryside.

"I think I should go where I have always been the happiest," said Beatrix.

~

It wasn't long afterward that Beatrix stood, alone and unchaperoned, on a hilltop in the Lake District, drinking in the power and the peace of the exquisite and spectacular view from Hill Top Farm. A short while later, she walked down the drive towards the gate. The "For Sale" sign still stood at the entrance. Beatrix picked up a stone, knocked the sign off the gate and took it with her.

Chapter Fourteen

A door opened in the simple bookcase-lined office of a country lawyer. Beatrix was ushered in by a clerk.

"Miss Potter, sir."

"Mr. Heelis?" said Beatrix.

A huge leather chair turned round revealing a now somewhat heavy-set man who seemed more likely to be found outdoors than in a lawyer's office. On seeing Beatrix, William Heelis's face broke into a huge smile. He was still, twenty years and a few pounds later, a remarkably handsome man.

"So it is you!" said Mr. Heelis. "You're the young lady buying Hill Top Farm. I am indeed most happy to hear it."

"How do you know of my intentions, Mr. Heelis?" said Beatrix.

"You live in the vast anonymity of London, madam," said Heelis. "Here in a small country town, everyone knows everything. Be warned."

"Are you telling me that moving to the country in order to find privacy is a lost cause?" said Beatrix.

"Not at all," said Heelis. "One can live a very private life in Sawrey. It's just that everyone in town will know about it."

Beatrix laughed. It occurred to her that she had not laughed in a very long time. "I'm wondering, Mr. Heelis, if you are in a position to act as solicitor for the purchase?" said Beatrix.

"I had hoped that might be your purpose," said William. "More than hoped, truth to tell. That farm . . ."

"How is it you know Hill Top so well?" said Beatrix.

"Raised on that farm," said William. "Swam in the lake, played hide-and-seek in the haymow with Master Charles. Rumor has it – dare I speak the words – that you intend to keep it as a working farm."

"Indeed, yes," said Beatrix. "I've asked Mr. Cannon to remain in residence to run it. I shall renovate the tenant's cottage for him."

"'Hallelujah!' he said quietly," said William.

Beatrix was taken aback. "So my decision meets with your approval?"

"Times are hard here, miss," said William. "So many farmers can't make a go of it. We locals weep. Every day, lovely English farmland chopped up for small houses. There are two other farms in jeopardy adjoining the very property you are buying."

"Is it so?" said Beatrix. "And are they for sale too?"

"Yes, they are," said William. He looked at her, suddenly realizing the implication of her question. "Is that of interest to you?"

"It could be so," said Beatrix. "Perhaps."

William Heelis made no attempt to hide his eagerness. "Would you like to see them? I can show them to you, if you like."

Beatrix rebuffed his friendliness. "I'm sure estate agent Hubbard will be happy to show them to me." This caused a small chill to fall over the room. So Beatrix went on, "Mr. Heelis, I haven't told you why I chose you to represent me."

"I should be interested to know."

"I selected you because I recall that land preservation was a special interest of yours. I intend at my death to donate Hill Top Farm to the new land association, the National Trust."

William Heelis's mouth fell open. "Have you dropped from heaven, Miss Potter?"

~

The Potter house in London was suddenly overrun with workmen. The movers had come to move Beatrix's belongings to her new home. Her room was filled with packing cases. All her books, drawings, stuffed animals and animal cages had been packed away and removed. The furniture was being carried out.

Beatrix had chosen to pack her artwork herself, with the help of one special packing man who had been assigned just to her. Beatrix took her framed pictures of Benjamin Bouncer off the wall, wrapped each separately in cloth and handed them to her helper to place in a packing case.

In her head, Beatrix replayed an exchange of letters from that morning.

The first was a letter from F. Warne and Co, which read:

> *My dear Miss Potter,*
> *May I call on you soon to discuss your future plans for*

publishing with F. Warne and Co.? The thought occurs
that it might be time for The Rabbits' Christmas Party?
        Yours sincerely,
            Harold Warne

Beatrix had dashed off a short note in reply. But somehow the note seemed of more significance than its simple content. And so she reread the notes in her mind. Her note said:

> *Dear Mr. Warne,*
>   *I am moving to the country. I have sent you all the stories I have written and I have no more ready to publish. Nor do I intend writing more in the near future. As for The Rabbits' Christmas Party, I have destroyed the manuscript and the plates. It is my wish that that story never be published.*
>   *Yours sincerely,*
>   *H. B. Potter*

Beatrix took the drawing of Jemima Puddle-duck off the wall. She remembered how Norman had leaned close to examine it. "Flirt," said Beatrix to Jemima, and wrapped her in a cloth.

Rupert Potter had been sitting in his own room, trying, he told himself, to sort through his photographs, but trying even harder not to hear the thumps and bangs that told him thunderously that his household was falling apart. Then Cox brought in the morning post.

Shortly afterward, Rupert went to Beatrix's room. Beatrix looked up at her father as he entered. He seemed suddenly old.

"Why is it necessary to leave your home?" Rupert said.

"It's not a choice, Father."

Rupert felt a sudden wave of regret pass through him. "Beatrix, if I could undo . . . anything . . ."

"There is nothing to undo. It has nothing to do with you, Father. Or Mother. I must go . . . on my own."

Rupert hesitated, then took a letter from his inside pocket. "Your move to the country has inspired Bertram to share some news. It seems your brother has been married – secretly – for seven years! To a Scots farm girl. Did you know this?"

Beatrix said gently, "No, Father. I knew about the girl, but not about the marriage."

Rupert looked at the letter with a kind of disbelief. "Bertram says we must leave you alone to find your own life, as he has." Rupert's shoulders sank. He looked into his daughter's eyes, then turned away. "I do not understand. Anything," he said.

He walked from the room.

From a shelf, Beatrix picked up a framed photo, taken by Rupert, of Beatrix and Bertram, aged twelve and seven, Beatrix immaculately neat, Bertram disheveled.

"Married? Oh, Bertie," said Beatrix.

She wrapped the photograph in a cloth and placed it in a crate.

"Life moves on, Bertie. Whether we like it or not."

∼

A cart bearing the sign "Movers of Fine Furniture" drove away from the newly renovated Hill Top Farm, leaving

Beatrix alone on the cobbled roadway. She turned and went inside.

The furniture was in place inside the crisp, freshly painted rustic house, but the rooms were still filled with a daunting supply of unopened packing crates. Beatrix looked around at the empty rooms. My, she thought, rooms are silent when one lives alone.

Then she clapped her hands and with sudden energy opened a crate. It happened to be a crate filled with children's doll versions of her creations. The soft dolls had been pressed down so that as the crate opened they seemed to pop up out of the box.

Beatrix took out two stuffed animals and showed them the room.

"Look, my friends: this will be your new home. I told you when we ventured into the world, we could not know where our adventure would lead. It has led us here. No tears."

She turned to place the toys on the mantel. Behind her, other stuffed animals, dolls of Peter Rabbit, Mrs. Tiggy-winkle, Squirrel Nutkin and a few other characters, their heads having popped up out of the crate, seemed to be looking around the room. Their glass eyes seemed frightened.

Beatrix found that the mantel was too narrow to hold the stuffed toys. She turned around, the two toys still in her hands.

"But where am I to put you?" she said.

She looked around the empty room. You can only go where you belong, she thought.

Her shoulders suddenly sagged.

The window ledge was wide enough to hold the two toys, so she put them there, backwards so that they stared out at the farmyard. Then she went back to the crate, pressed the soft toys back into it, and closed it tight.

~

Beatrix settled into Hill Top Farm. Each morning, a rooster's crow woke her in her new bedroom. She rose, dressed, went downstairs and breakfasted alone. Alone didn't seem nearly so bad here in the country, she thought, in her own farm.

One morning she noticed a package beside the door that someone had delivered. She opened it and found a book with a letter attached to it. The letter was from Harold Warne, and it read:

My dear Miss Potter,
    I enclose herewith a proof copy of Pierre Lapin. This French translation, along with the proposed German translation and your first publication in America should bring you a vast new audience. But, may I say, what the world is truly awaiting is a new Beatrix Potter book. Can you tell me if . . .

Beatrix folded the letter and didn't finish reading it.

Instead, she went out of the house into a beautiful spring morning, where, in the farmyard, the farmhands were already at their duties.

At the pigsty, Beatrix's tenant, Mr. Cannon, was bent over a fence admiring the night's arrivals, several newly born piglets.

"Handsome lot, wouldn't you say?" said Mr. Cannon, as Beatrix came up beside him.

"Indeed so," said Beatrix. "Have you named them yet?"

Mr. Cannon poured some mash in for the sow. "Now, it isn't often we give them names, Miss Potter. Makes it a bit hard come slaughtering time."

"Well, they are *my* firstborn and I shall name them," said Beatrix. She pointed out each piglet.

"I would name that one Pigson, and Pigroot, that one over there Piggery, the very distinguished gentleman with the white spats, he will be Pigling, and, um – that little black one is the sow, isn't it? – she shall be Pig-wig. In honor of Mr. Dickens."

"And who would that be, mum?" said Mr. Cannon.

Beatrix suddenly realized how far she had moved from city life. She patted Mr. Cannon on the hand. "Just a gentleman who writes books," she said.

William Heelis walked out of the field, having come to Hill Top the back way, through the woods over the hill. He entered the farmyard.

"Halloo, Miss Potter!" he cried.

"Halloo yourself, Mr. Heelis," called Beatrix. "To what do I owe this pleasure?"

"I've come with a message," said William. "Mr. Hubbard is ill and will be unable to show you the neighboring farms today."

"Oh dear," said Beatrix. "It isn't serious, I hope."

William Heelis answered dryly, "Chronic illness. Recurs several times a month, usually after a night at the Rose and Crown."

"I see," said Beatrix.

Mr. Heelis hesitated just the slightest before pressing on. "Mr. Hubbard asked whether I might show you the properties instead, seeing as few around know the farms as well as I. I agreed with alacrity. With your permission, of course."

Something in Beatrix made her resist the effusive Mr. Heelis. "I can wait till Mr. Hubbard recovers," she said. "Thank you for your trouble, Mr. Heelis."

William Heelis was crestfallen, but tried to conceal it. "Perhaps another day," he said, and turned to leave. Then he turned back. "John, tell Miss Potter how well I know this land."

Mr. Cannon was a blunt country farmer to whom people turned for the truth, because he didn't know how to be clever. "Ah, Mr. William knows these whereabouts better'n any Jack-the-lad, that's for sure, Miss Potter."

Beatrix hesitated. In her head she suddenly heard Norman's voice, inviting her to visit a printing house. She had said no then – at first. Why was she once again feeling the same impulse?

"Mr. Heelis, I should be pleased to have so knowledgeable a guide to escort me," she said. "I'll just get my shawl."

William could not hide his pleasure. He called after her, "Your restoration of the house is the talk of Sawrey, Miss Potter."

Beatrix looked at him. "Come in, if you like," she said. "You can tell me if it's as you remember it."

When he entered the house, William was gobsmacked. The rooms were exactly as he remembered them from his childhood, except now fresh painted and new. But the parlor of the farmhouse was stacked with framed pictures, sketches, watercolors, nature studies, drawings – ten deep in places, stacks and stacks of art. There would never be enough wall space for them.

"Oh my! Oh my, my!" he said. He studied the drawings: toadstools, leaves, rabbits, dead birds, a magnification of a butterfly's wing.

"Do you still love paintings, Mr. Heelis?" said Beatrix.

"Aye, indeed so," said William. "Art seems a true Wonder to me. One of the greatest Wonders. I can't understand how a body creates it." He leafed through more pictures and then, unaccountably, burst out laughing.

Beatrix looked at him curiously. Laughter was not a response she anticipated.

"I think I'm ready now," she said, wrapping her shoulders in her shawl.

Beside the front door, William saw a framed painting of Peter Rabbit, one of the few pictures Beatrix had found space for on the wall. He leaned in close and talked to it. Beatrix felt a spasm pass through her. William Heelis looked just like Norman examining the picture of Jemima Puddle-duck.

"Well now, Peter," said William to the painting, "how are you taking to your new home? I know it's not London, but Hill Top might suit a young rabbit better!"

He turned to Beatrix. "Peter seems to be taking to the place."

Beatrix smiled.

"As am I, Mr. Heelis. Now . . . the road."

They emerged from the house.

"Are you writing any new stories, Miss Potter?" said William, as they started down the lane. "You once told me a story about a duck. I was stunned to come across it all in print in a bookshop."

"Yes, I should have thanked you for that long ago," said Beatrix. "I am not writing at present, no," she said, "but I think . . ." a cloud crossed her face, ". . . I think I may again soon. I am beginning to feel the need."

"I'm sure we'll all be happy for that," said William.

Hill Top Farm disappeared into the distance.

Chapter Fifteen

So it was that Beatrix Potter and William Heelis found themselves once more on a long walk in the English countryside, traveling by unexpected and out-of-the-way pathways to visit Wonders. But these Wonders were not obscure and erotic flora. They were English farms – some fallen into disrepair, but each one more breathtaking and extraordinary than the next. Walking beside William, even walking at a certain distance from him, Beatrix could not help feeling an old and recognizable sensation of electricity. Mr. Heelis still strode out powerfully as if nothing could stop him. And it still seemed as if at any moment he could burst into song. Walking with him, Beatrix began to feel as if she were two people – herself, an unmarried adult woman of a certain age, proceeding somehow with a life transformed by love and anaesthetized by grief, and at the same time, in flashes of sensations that she fought against feeling, she was a sixteen-year-old girl overwhelmed by her first real crush.

These were not feelings she wished to feel.

William led Beatrix on a shortcut through a wood and they emerged to see a small farmhouse in a meadow filled with wild lilies.

"This is Fell Foot," said William. "Owned by Mr. James Cargill. Hasn't paid Thornbury's for last year's seed."

They walked down a narrow country lane with high

hedges on either side and reached a gate that led into a millhouse farm enchantingly situated beside a brook studded with clumps of jonquils and iris.

"Craven's Mill," said William. "Of late, owned by the Misses Prudence and Dora Craven. But Miss Prudence passed on and Dora went to live with her cousin. The farm seems to be in the hands of a nephew in Yorkshire who doesn't know what to do with it."

They walked up a winding lane to a rustic cottage built into the ruins of a tiny ancient castle. This farm was larger than Hill Top, and as they approached it, Beatrix and Mr. Heelis found that the house sat upon an even more beautiful vista than Hill Top itself.

"Castle Farm," said William. "At this moment unoccupied. If someone doesn't buy it soon, it will begin to collapse. They say some of the house was built in 1486."

"One hundred and sixty acres, you say?" asked Beatrix.

"Adjoining yours," said William. "This is the farm I dreamed of buying for myself. But on the wages of a country lawyer . . ."

Beatrix walked a distance away, drinking in the view. "It's remarkable," she said. "Lying fallow! Such splendor."

"Not a bad place to park a bit of Peter Rabbit's lettuce, I dare say," said William.

He set down his rucksack. "Now then, Miss Potter, please tell me that all this walking has stirred up your appetite. For myself, I'm famished. And, against just this occurrence, I've taken the liberty of packing a few essentials."

Beatrix felt a resistance rise in her again. "For a picnic lunch?"

"You might say," said William.

Beatrix did not understand the emotion that coursed through her. She suddenly felt — unaccountably — angry. She wanted to run home.

"Mr. Heelis, you are extending yourself much too far on my behalf," she said. "No luncheon, thank you. And please don't do such things again."

She paused. Mr. Heelis had done nothing untoward. Why did she feel such a need to be rude to him? It was ridiculous.

"In fact, I *am* quite hungry," said Beatrix. "A picnic was . . . very thoughtful of you, Mr. Heelis."

William relaxed, and Beatrix saw once again the boyish grin that had captivated her more than twenty years earlier.

He opened the rucksack and took out a checkered cloth. "What say we sit at the well, have a bit of bread and sausage, and imagine that it's 1486, and we're sitting on this knoll planning to build a house. What kind of house shall it be, madam?"

Beatrix did not pick up her cue.

"I think," said William, after a moment. "I think we should build a castle." He waved his hand towards the cottage. "Over there, don't you think? A . . . small castle, of course."

"I'm not good at pretending, Mr. Heelis," said Beatrix. "It's something I only do when I work."

William was surprised at her response. He looked around with great seriousness. "Build a castle here?" he said. "What a curious idea? Whatever made me think of it? But . . ." he smiled again, ". . . I like it!"

Beatrix knew right then why she had grown angry.

She was not going to let Mr. William Heelis charm her, or get near to her, in any way.

~

Some time later, a carriage drove up the road to Castle Farm. The coachman jumped out and helped Beatrix, then Mr. and Mrs. Potter, to descend.

Mrs. Potter looked out at the spectacular vista. "Well!" she said. "This is indeed the Lake District at its most magnificent! Is this what you'd like your father to rent for us next summer?"

"No, Mother," said Beatrix. "I own it. I bought it this morning. It's mine."

"Is it!" exclaimed Rupert. "Another farm for me to photograph! What a thoughtful daughter I have!" The coachman was lifting down heavy cases from the carriage. "Careful there with the camera!" Rupert called out.

Beatrix spoke to her mother. "I intend to renovate the main house. In years to come, should you ever become too infirm for London, you will live here."

Mrs. Potter huffed. "I will do no such thing."

"If I am to look after you," said Beatrix, "you will have to be nearby."

Rupert, setting his camera on its tripod, began a fit of coughing. "Are you all right, Father?" said Beatrix.

"I'm fine," said Rupert, coughing again as he unpacked the flash powder that would, in a few years, kill him.

Mrs. Potter's voice became even louder. "Move here, all year? Never! Never, never, never!"

Beatrix suddenly noticed that somehow her parents

both seemed older. She went to her mother and took her by the hand. "Come, Mother, pose for Father and then I'll show you the house."

Mrs. Potter, sputtering, set herself in a rigid position and faced the camera. "Where do you get the money to buy all these farms?"

"I'm an artist, Mother," said Beatrix. "A writer and artist. People buy my work."

Rupert set his focus. "Our daughter's famous, Helen. You're the only person in the world who doesn't know it," he said. He ran out to stand beside them, froze, and the camera flashed.

～

That evening at Hill Top Farm, Beatrix was alone. A fire glowed in the hearth. She had spent the morning in Mr. Heelis's office, arranging to purchase Castle Farm. Mr. Heelis had been efficient, meticulous, forceful, articulate, yet all the while remained cheerful and even witty. There were an endless number of details to discuss, which kept her in William's company seemingly forever – but all day long, during all the time she was with Mr. Heelis, Beatrix felt a growing desire, almost amounting to a panic, to get home and begin to write something.

On the writing table before her was yet another letter from Harold Warne. It read:

My dear Miss Potter,
    It has now been almost a year since the last new Beatrix Potter story. Have you given any further thought to . . .

Beatrix took pen in hand to write a reply.

Dear Mr. Warne,
The seed in your recent letter has found fertile soil. For quite a while, I have not felt ready to write a new Tale. I think now it is time to return to my — she searched for the right word — to my trade. Perhaps you shall soon have the new manuscript you request.
Yours sincerely,
H. B. Potter

Beatrix folded the letter and placed it in an envelope. Then she went to a cabinet and took out paints, ink, and her sketchbook. With an effort, as if the cover were heavy, she opened the sketchbook. This simple act, preparing to draw, which used to be her life, now seemed full of peril.

The room was silent.

Beatrix stared at the blank page. Nothing came. She raised her hands to her pursed lips and thought. What did she know about? Was there some idea here at the farm?

She took up her pen and dipped it in ink.

She began to draw: a picture of a gentlemanly pig in spats, waistcoat and a jaunty hat. Then she lettered a book title, saying the words out loud to herself as she wrote.

"*The Tale of Pigling Bland,*" she said.

On the page, the drawing took shape. Beatrix tinted the drawing with color, and then tore out the page and began a second drawing. Pigling Bland seemed to jump from page to page as his story formed. It was like the old days — a jolly Tale forming itself before her eyes, this one of a country gentleman pig, dressed in his Sunday best, who had grown too big for his farm and was being sent to market to find employment elsewhere.

Beatrix drew feverishly. As had happened when she was very young, words came to her in a verse, and she spoke them out loud.

"Pigling Bland, Pigling Bland
        Felt that he might be forsaken
He didn't want to be lonely, and
        He didn't want to be bacon.
So he donned his jacket, his Sunday best
        And the waistcoat that had such charm
And he put on his hat and buttoned his vest
        And ran away from the farm."

As the tale unfolded, Beatrix's face became more and more pained. The more she drew the more pronounced the pain grew. She began to wince at endearing childlike elements she once reveled in.

"Pigs in coats!" she said aloud. "I don't think the world needs any more of that." She tore up the drawing she was working on. Then she added, "And no verse!" She tore off the page with the rhymed lines and ripped that up too.

But when she started a new page, she once again put a coat on Pigling Bland.

She proceeded with her story well into the night, her pen flicking across each page, drawing the story as fast as she could invent it. One phrase from the story kept repeating itself:

As Pigling Bland traveled toward Market Town, through adventure after adventure, he sang to himself:

"I must go off on my own, my own,
I must go off on my own."

Beatrix began to sing along with him.

"I must go off on my own, my own,
I must go off on my own."

In the story, on the first day of his solo journey, Pigling
Bland got lost and was sheltered for the night by a seemingly
friendly, but somehow ominous, farmer. It was clear that
something life-threatening was about to happen to Pigling.
But as he settled in for the night, Beatrix suddenly stopped
drawing. She sat still. She put down her pen. The expected
turn of story somehow did not seem interesting to her.

"Pigling Bland," she said. "Where should your story
go now?"

Pigling Bland looked up from the page, half-drawn.
He had no suggestions. He gestured that it was up to her.

Beatrix picked up her pen again. She began to draw.

Into the farmhouse room in which Pigling Bland was
sleeping came a new character, a beautiful girl-pig named
Pig-wig, who had black hair, and a very sensible attitude
about her. Pigling Bland looked at Pig-wig, and instantly
liked her. Why was she here? Pigling asked.

Pig-wig informed Pigling Bland that she, like all pigs,
was being raised by the farmer to be made into bacon,
hams, and sausages. Pigling was horrified. "Why on earth
don't you run away?" he exclaimed. "I shall after supper,"
said Pig-wig. Pigling decided to run away with her.

The next morning before dawn, they took off down the

road. They met a grocer in his cart who seemed about to take them to market – but they eluded him.

Nothing much happened to them after that – except that on the last page Pigling Bland and Pig-wig were running away together over hill and dale, Pig-wig's petticoats all a-flutter, free at last:

"They came to the river, they came to the bridge –
    They crossed it hand in hand –
Then over the hills and far away
    She danced with Pigling Bland."

It was dawn. Beatrix put down her paintbrush. Tears were streaming down her cheeks.

~

"It's a love story, Beatrix," said Millie. Millie had come up from London for a visit. She had Beatrix's manuscript in her hand. "You've written a love story. For children."

"I don't know where it came from, Millie," said Beatrix. "Well, you and I both know, of course. But I suddenly couldn't write an innocent little story again. It's gone."

Millie held up the manuscript. "It's hardly gone. This story is delightful."

"No, Millie – gone," said Beatrix. "Look at these packing crates. They are filled with my books and my dolls and my plates and my placemats and my drawings – I can't unpack them. I have no room for them. In my house. In my life. Millie, I don't think I'll ever write a story again. This was my last."

"That would be a tragedy," said Millie. "How could you ever give up a gift?"

"Life has a way of deciding things for you, Millie," said Beatrix. "Pretending no longer makes me happy. Maybe I'm not meant to be happy any more. Not in that way."

"You baffle me so," said Millie. She studied Beatrix's face.

"Beatrix," Millie said, "remember your Christmas party, when I told you to marry Norman! I often think, what if I hadn't encouraged you? Would I have saved you all this pain?"

"You mean," said Beatrix, "what if God offered me a choice: Beatrix, you can go back in time, you will not meet Norman, you will not find love – *but*, you will never feel this loneliness and pain. Oh Millie, I would choose the loneliness! I would choose the pain!"

Tears suddenly flooded Millie's eyes.

"Millie, what's the matter?" said Beatrix. "Why are you crying?"

"Because I don't know what you're talking about," she said.

Beatrix held Millie in her arms.

~

All through that night, Beatrix found herself replaying the great events of her life. It was as if for the first time she saw her life in total instead of as a collection of moments. She remembered the day when she found she could draw, the day she learned to paint, the first day she created a story. She was always a lonely girl, but if there was a void in her of any kind, art filled it. She never felt her life lacked for anything when she was drawing something.

Then came the day when a friend who had once been her governess, Annie Moore, wrote to tell her that her six-year-old son Noel was ill and would have to stay in bed for some time. Beatrix sat down intending to write him a letter, but she remembered a story from her childhood, and what she actually wrote was:

> *My dear Noel,*
> *I don't know what to write to you, so I shall tell you a tale about four little rabbits whose names were Flopsy, Mopsy, Cotton-tail and Peter . . .*

She sent off the story and received a charming thank-you letter from Noel in reply. The emotion she felt on reading Noel's reply was remarkable. She felt she had touched someone. Cloaked in the safety of a story, she had sent herself to another person, and that person – even though it was just a child – had responded to her.

She felt connected, and in a very subtle way, less alone. And so when the opportunity arose with Noel's brothers and sisters, she did it again.

> *My dear Freda,*
> *Because you are fond of fairy-tales, and have been ill, I have made you a story all for yourself . . .*

> *My dear Norah,*
> *I dare say you are big enough now to want a letter, so this is the story of how Squirrel Nutkin lost his tail . . .*

The sensation was so pleasant she decided to have *The Tale of Peter Rabbit* printed, so that she could give it more easily to friends. Each time she presented her gift, she felt the same subtle thrill, a link, a connection, a release from her separateness. Is there something in human beings that leads them toward contact with others? she thought. Are human beings not meant to live alone?

Then came the day she showed her small volume, and a few other stories, to Canon Rawnsley, the vicar, who said the fateful words that changed her life: "You should publish them." After which he found her a publisher, and she met Norman Warne, and left the safety of her protected life forever. With Norman, she felt joy. She had never felt joy before, the kind that took over her body, transformed her soul, and made her feel that she would never again touch the ground. And she encountered grief, a pain of such profundity that it entered her being, overwhelmed her body and made her feel that she could never – ever – go on. It was such intense grief that she longed to release herself from her suffering, to run away, to retreat again into the safety of a fantasy world inside her head. But she could not run away. The stories she created no longer protected her. And astonishingly, she found that she did not want to run away. Because it was the pain she felt that linked her to Norman. And she did not wish to release her hold on it, or on him.

In the orange glow from the fading embers of the fire, Beatrix looked around her new home. She had opened the crate of stuffed animals and had placed them on the table facing her, so they could all see.

"Life moves us on, my friends, and we do not

determine where it takes us," she said out loud. "And sometimes we must leave precious things behind, willy-nilly, whether we want to or not. You have been my friends for as long as I can remember. But I must move on. And I can't take you with me."

The dolls stared back with fixed glass eyes.

"All I can hope is that you'll understand, and – perhaps, wish me well."

~

Beatrix heard the voice of William Heelis, outside. It was morning. She had fallen asleep in an armchair.

"Halloo, Miss Potter," called William.

"Halloo, Mr. Heelis!" Beatrix opened the door to him.

William kicked mud off his shoe before entering. "Today's farm is a little further away. Thought perhaps we'd get an early start."

"If you say so, Mr. Heelis," said Beatrix. "I'll only be a moment."

William began once again to examine the stacks of paintings and drawings that filled the parlor. Beatrix looked at him, so intent.

"Mr. Heelis," she said, "when you saw my drawings that first day, why did you laugh?"

"Well," said William, "truth to tell, it's because I discovered a painting of the fungi I showed you all those years ago. So finely drawn! Did you go back?"

"Only in my mind, Mr. Heelis. In my mind, I went back many times." Beatrix suddenly felt she had revealed too much. "To get the painting just right," she added.

"I believe in representing nature as it is."

"Oh yes, like rabbits in jackets," William said wickedly.

"Now you are using your lawyer skill on me. My stories are another thing. Am I not to be allowed a shred of mystery?"

"Oh, you have plenty of that. A woman alone, buying a house away from everyone. No father, no husband . . . No solicitor, perish the thought! Just a tableful of creations to keep her company. But what do I know – perhaps that's enough."

"Time will tell, Mr. Heelis."

"So it will, Miss Potter, but it won't wait. So we'd better get on."

"On to where, Mr. Heelis?"

"That's entirely up to you, Miss Potter."

"So it is, Mr. Heelis," Beatrix said. "So it is."

On an impulse she took several more of her stuffed dolls, as many as she could, and added them to the dolls she had placed in the window. Then she joined Mr. Heelis and they went out into the morning sun.

"Miss Potter," said Heelis, as they started down the road, "this is rather difficult to say, but . . . well . . . Do you remember that I once confessed to a weakness for country dancing? Well, the Historical Society brings fiddlers to Sawrey every now and again, and . . . Have you learned to dance, Miss Potter?"

"I do not dance, Mr. Heelis."

"Oh. Ah well. Pity," said William. "On our way then."

Beatrix hesitated.

"I had one lesson once," said Beatrix.

"Did you now," said William. "And how did it go?"

"It was the most beautiful moment of my life," said Beatrix.

William was taken aback by the answer. "You're a deep well, Miss Potter," he said. "But I suppose that's what makes you an artist." He smiled at her. "Perhaps you'd like another dance lesson then? As I say, I'm considered quite a proficient teacher."

"Or I could come with you and watch," said Beatrix. "I'm sure a country dance in Sawrey is something not to miss."

"It is that, Miss Potter," said William. "Well. Plenty of time to discuss dancing later. Now, time to visit farms."

Beatrix looked back over her shoulder. The windows of Hill Top were filled with Beatrix's creations, and they seemed to be waving goodbye.

"What are you looking at?" asked William.

"Women who have been alone too long start to see things, Mr. Heelis. I'm only a little batty, I assure you."

She raised her fingers to her lips and blew a kiss back to the house.

"Thank you, friends."

William looked at the house. What he saw was just a few stuffed animals propped up in a window. William thought for a moment.

"I suppose I'm man enough to accept a few eccentricities. And speaking of personal quirks, Miss Potter, I have one too. How would you feel about calling me William, instead of all this infernal Mr. Heelis? I feel like an undertaker."

They continued down the path, walking into one of the most beautiful countrysides on the face of the earth. Walking together.

Afterword

Beatrix Potter and William Heelis were married on October 14, 1913.

Beatrix died in 1943; William Heelis two years later.

She published only a few additional stories after her marriage.

The Tale of Peter Rabbit remains the bestselling children's picture book of all time.